The Flamer

The Flamer

BEN ROGERS

BAOBAB PRESS
RENO, NV

First Baobab Press Printing

ISBN-13: 978-1-936097-17-3
ISBN-10: 1-936097-17-6

Library of Congress Control Number: 2018950305

Baobab Press
121 California Avenue
Reno, Nevada 89509
www.baobabpress.com

For those who nurture, especially
Jim, Sandy, and Jill

FOREWORD

When I was growing up, all the books I read were set in the same place: *elsewhere*. That's where stories happened. That's where writers came from. Also, all the writers were dead. You'd never see one.

I discovered *The City of Trembling Leaves* by Walter Van Tilburg Clark when I was in high school. "This is the story of the lives and loves of Timothy Hazard," it begins, "and so, indirectly, a token biography of Reno." It read like *my* biography. Tim, just like me, attended Reno High School, where he took sixth-period physics, played on the tennis team, and had a serious girlfriend. The writing was exquisite, the page count gravitational, the accolades legit. This was *literature*, despite being set in my hometown and having the most pedestrian of all possible protagonists: me.

I felt grateful to Clark for capturing the truth of my city—its beauty and its blight, both. For getting it right. As, of course, he would. He lived in these hills. Mt. Rose wasn't a mountain to him, it was a religion. He was preaching to the choir.

I felt grateful for the story too. Clark elevated my existence by taking Tim's so seriously.

The City of Trembling Leaves made me want to write. Or, *gave me permission to*.

The book was originally published by Random House in 1945.

The edition I read was the one re-published in 1991 by the University of Nevada Press, with a foreword by the press's founder, Robert Laxalt. In it, Laxalt recounts a snowy drive up Geiger Grade to meet Clark at his home in Virginia City. Laxalt was looking for a mentor, and found one. Over drinks at a saloon, Clark jotted down the titles of seventeen novels Laxalt might read to help him in his writing. Laxalt kept that slip of paper all his life.

I immediately co-opted Clark as my own guru, and took it upon myself to read those books too. I checked off three I'd already read for school: *Heart of Darkness* by Joseph Conrad, *The Red Badge of Courage* by Stephen Crane, and *Crime and Punishment* by Fyodor Dostoevsky. Over the coming years, I worked my way through the list. I was confounded (Faulkner), titillated (*Lady Chatterly*, Clark having insisted on the once-banned original edition), and broadened by foreign voices (Turgenev, Rölvaag, Hamsun). There were books I *knew* I'd find boring (*Death Comes For the Archbishop*), only to be proven stupid.

I wish I could say I've read every book on that list. I have (so far) read fourteen of them, and promise I will try to pick off the final three. Here's what happened though. Clark's prescription was my gateway drug. Soon, I was mainlining Hemingway. Joyce. Irving, Wolff, Eggers, Tyler, Franzen, Stegner, Mitchell, Haruf, Doerr, Morrison. McCarthy. Vonnegut. Every writer led to another. "So it goes."

I started writing.

Years later, I found a way to actually have lunch with Mr. Laxalt. By then, I had finally "discovered" him too—this giant of letters living just a few miles away, in Washoe Valley. I loved his books. I was a fanboy. He would be the first novelist I'd ever met.

He wore sweatpants to the restaurant. (No tweed? No elbow patches?) He hadn't shaved in a few days. I watched as this wordsmith I so revered stacked pickles on a hamburger, then sucked his fingers clean. He dragged droopy fries through a puddle of ketchup. The napkin tucked into his collar made him look so much more person-like than I might have expected, or, at that time, preferred. He did not resemble the statue of "Papa" in Pamplona. Turns out, writers aren't bronze busts. Mr. Laxalt—Bob, as his friends called him—was incredibly...warm.

I'd come to him more for instruction than inspiration. Kid to magician: *how do you do that? I can keep secrets.* I'd seen a picture of his writing desk in the May/June 1998 issue of *Nevada Magazine.* It was a dark, stained wood—secretary-style with drawers and all, some of which could be locked with a key. The desk, at least, looked just the way I wanted it to. A green lamp. Papers with his handwriting. His cross-outs. His Pulitzer-worthy Post-its. A mug of coffee . (Did he take sugar?) A pair of glasses. A pocket watch dangling from a drawer handle. (Did it tick? Loudly? Did he time his sessions?)

And, oh!, the trusty typewriter. A blue Royal. A fossil. There was a page arcing back from its rollers and on the page were The Words.

The keypads had stiff metal stems that surely required mightier fingers than my computer keyboard. I visualized him typing—each keystroke bringing to life levers and hinges, tiny arms hammering home their indelible black handprints in wet ink on an actual paper page sliding leftward and then, BANG! Hard return. New line. Letters into words into paragraphs separated by sips of tepid coffee. There was not a trace of ketchup to be seen on those sacred keys.

I asked him: Doesn't using a typewriter make editing hard? (My word processor let me re-work sentences for hours, the way one might train obstinate, over-groomed poodles.)

I choose my words very carefully, he said to me.

Okay, I thought. Note to self.

After grad school, my wife and I did a stint in Tennessee and then Los Angeles for my job before returning home to Reno. It felt right to be back, amongst our people, our mountains, our memories. That's when I started writing *The Flamer*—an ode to my formative years, whether I recognized it at the time or not.

Clark called Reno the "City of Trembling Leaves," but a few pages later he also called it "a city of adolescence, a city of dissonant themes, sawing against each other with a kind of piercing beauty like that of a fourteen-year-old girl or a seventeen-year-old boy, the beauty of everything promised and nothing resolved." What a fertile and befitting backdrop for my little bildungsroman!

And what a great city to write in, and about! There are so many great voices and open ears in Northern Nevada. Christopher Coake—who eventually became the Clark to my Laxalt (though I have not been a fraction as fruitful a mentee), and whose encouragement and counsel surely saved *The Flamer* from the fate of my first novel (a file box in my basement)—recently championed the creation of a fantastic MFA program in creative writing at the University of Nevada (among whose ranks there are surely latent Laxalts). There's an annual lit crawl. There's an ever-expanding pantheon in the Nevada Writers Hall of Fame. Mark Twain—a member of the Hall—might say that reports of our region as a literary desert are greatly exaggerated.

I like to go see visiting authors when they come to town, often as part of the Robert Laxalt Distinguished Writer Program. Invariably, they remark on what a pleasant surprise it is to find such a thriving literary scene here. They'll tell us we don't know how lucky we are to have a bookstore like Sundance.

I think I know, though. I'm incredibly grateful to Baobab (a press named for a tree) for replanting this little book where it belongs, amongst the trembling leaves.

From trees come books.

- Ben Rogers
Reno, Nevada
September 2017

The Flamer

PROLOGUE

On the morning of January 21, 1985, a Lockheed L-188A Electra four-engine turboprop took off from Reno, Nevada. The plane carried six crew members and 65 passengers. Among them were both George Lamsons, Junior and Senior, ages 17 and 41. When the plane lifted, stray engine vibrations transmitted uncontrollably to a propeller and then to a wing, causing the plane to flutter in midair. The pilot powered back. Moments later the Electra fell out of the sky. It skidded across a field, then left the ground again, jumping a 20-foot-wide irrigation ditch before finally sliding to a halt in the parking lot of an RV dealership, where it was engulfed in the flames of burning jet fuel and exploding motor home propane tanks.

Fire crews arriving soon thereafter found George Jr. sitting smack in the middle of Reno's main drag, South Virginia Street, still strapped to his chair, conscious and bearing no more than a few bumps and bruises. The other 70 people aboard died. True story.

A horrible, horrible story, retold here merely as a metaphor—

albeit an entirely disproportionate metaphor—for the boyhood of one Oby Brooks. Me. Hurled unscathed from what would otherwise have been a fiery end in Reno.

What went through George Jr.'s head as he sat in his chair in the middle of the street with his seatbelt still fastened low and tight? Probably a shock like few of us will ever know. But I bet that when he eventually caught his breath and had a moment to think, he was horrified and grateful and confused all at once.

Maybe he thanked God. In which case, here ends this horrible metaphor. My thanks are owed elsewhere, I think.

ONE

We were gathered on the frozen front lawn, watching black smoke billow from Mom and Dad's bathroom window. Ash settled over the northern hemisphere of the Weber, the windshield of our wood-paneled Wagoneer, my Nikes. Todd was still in his pajamas and I in my mood. We heard axe strokes inside the living room. The blades came hacking through the insulation and wood, followed closely by a pair of firemen who collapsed against one another in the driveway, chests heaving. Dad pulled me aside.

Oby, he said, finger-stirring a Bloody Mary. Straighten up. Keep an eye on your brother. I don't want you guys in the way.

I slipped his embrace and wandered past neighbors and family friends over to a fireman tending gauges on the pump truck to ask if he'd sound the air horn.

Little early for that, he said, and he gave me a lesson on hydrants instead. Told me never to play with matches.

Little late for that. I was in third grade. I knew things. I knew that strike-anywhere matches wore volatile little white yarmulkes.

I also knew that if we hadn't inherited our house from Grandpa

Robert we couldn't have afforded it. Nestled in the older section of Reno off Dartmouth Drive, the lot had a big backyard with a pond. Feisty swans patrolled the banks and kept the ducks at bay—the aristocracy of the neighborhood enforceable among its waterfowl. The house was cozy, with low ceilings and tiny bathrooms. There were small spaces to curl up in. But the heating system was shot and the roof leaked. The IRS allowed Dad to legally write off the value of the structure if he donated it to the Reno Fire Department for training purposes. So, the fire crew got a house to practice in, Dad got a tax break, and I got hosed.

They didn't just burn down the place. They tortured it. First they filled it with smoking barrels and crawled through rooms looking for a dummy so they could drag it out, over and over again. One of the rooms was where we ate Thanksgiving dinner, another where I played Atari. One room was mine.

Later that morning Todd and I took to playacting lopsided fight scenarios with the practice dummy. Its 200-pound lifelikeness outweighed us both combined, so its self-defense consisted of leg sweeps, sucker punches, and ankle biting. We kicked its ass a few dozen ways. A couple of times when I knee-bombed its ribcage, I pretended it was Dad.

Mom served the crew chili in sourdough bowls for lunch. In return they carried wood pallets and bales of hay into our house. The chief lit a flare and carried it with him through the front door with the solemnity of an altar boy. The sparkling wick cast ghoulish shadows over his face. I caught glimpses through the windows as the flare floated through the kitchen and into the dining room. It climbed the stairs. When the chief came back outside he was empty handed. The thing remained inside the house somewhere, biding its time. Hoses had been stationed on all sides of the house. The crew turned them on and off, pre-drenching our evergreens. The wind blew dead leaves around.

I glanced over at Mr. Ligon, Dad's boss at the bank. His little girls wore matching hats and gloves. The youngest saw me and ducked behind her sister, who gnawed a rope of licorice. Mr. Ligon brought out his video camera. Clenched between his teeth was one of the cigars Dad handed out. Mr. Ligon had the same perfect and immobile hair as a G.I. Joe doll. He turned the camera on me.

Whadya think, Oby? he said. Isn't this wild?

Wild, I said.

It's like a show, he said.

For you, Mr. Ligon, I thought. For you. Me, I crammed my stuff in a U-Haul a few months ago and moved to an apartment with shampooed carpet down by the Truckee River, but that shampoo smell went away. And the smells it had covered up came uncovered. While I'd managed to reuse their original thumbtack holes, my posters' sizes and orientations hadn't jibed with the walls the way they had in my room. They hadn't jibed at all, Mr. Ligon.

Now you can finally build a place to be proud of, Mr. Ligon said.

A plume of smoke was choking out the sun a little. An upstairs window cracked. Shards of glass fell to the frozen lawn and sizzled. One of the firemen standing behind me explained that at a certain temperature, most everything in a house becomes flammable and abruptly bursts into flame. There were a few seconds there when the house seemed to breathe in. I could feel it.

I'd prepared myself for that moment, to be enraged. But there wasn't time. The flames churned, hungry for everything. I could feel the heat on my cheeks and against my chest. Never had I seen or heard such restlessness as was alive in those flames. They were vines, enwrapping front-porch pillars. They were water, spilling out windows and up walls, disobeying gravity. Through the broken places in the wall I saw paint bubbling, the fire without mercy. Entire walls contorted, toppled. The firemen knocked down stray embers with spurts of water.

I stood 20 yards from the front door the whole time. Stairs wilted into what was once the living room. The house seemed made of paper, so flimsy was its resistance. A fireman offered Todd a shot manning the hose. He was too small for the powerful kick of the jet and so the fireman braced him. Together they aimed water at the burning walls, forcing them to fall.

The embers steamed and hissed. Flames recoiled to reveal a scaly, black carcass. A dragon was eating my house and I couldn't tear my eyes away.

Your turn, said the fireman, offering me the hose. We need to wet these flames down.

Oooh! Mom said. Give it a try, Oby.

I was gathering wood scraps from the yard and tossing them on the pile, just to watch the dragon eat.

No thank you, I said, going to fetch more wood.

This was the first time my house burned.

TWO

Mrs. Felton told us about Sodom and Gomorrah in Sunday school, how the angels urged Lot and his family to get the hell away and never look back. But Lot's wife looked back anyway. She saw the fire and brimstone rain upon the damned and for her disobedience was turned to a pillar of salt. I would have looked back, too. Anyone would have.

I was in fourth grade. I asked Mrs. Felton what brimstone was.

It's the same as sulfur, she said.

What's sulfur?

Oh, she said. Well, it smells like rotten eggs.

She handed out pictures. Turns out there really *are* balls of sulfur embedded in the ground near the Dead Sea, site of the doomed cities.

The Bible, she told us, is a history.

Perhaps, Mrs. Felton. Perhaps. But it seems to lack crucial details, which makes it all but useless to a boy of my persuasion, one left to find out on his own that sulfur, when sublimed, forms a fine yellow powder which can be mixed with charcoal and saltpeter to make gunpowder. Mrs. Felton, I realize your story about Sodom and Gomorrah was meant to teach us the importance of obeying the Lord, but for a chance to witness what may have been the fiercest firestorm ever unleashed on Earth, Lot's wife got a keen bargain.

Anyway, I asked Mom why we were Episcopalians.

Because we believe in what Episcopalians believe in, she said, pinning a pillowcase to her chest with her chin.

Like how Jesus came back, I said.

Right.

What about the Levys?

The Levys are Jewish.

Yeah. So, what do they think?

Jews don't believe Jesus was the savior, she said, setting down the pillowcase and pulling another out of the dryer. That's why Josh doesn't get Christmas presents. They celebrate Hanukkah.

Are Grandma Jane and Grandpa Murt Episcopalian?

You know *that*. You've been to church with Grandma and Grandpa.

It was kind of different.

Just longer, Mom said. But you knew the songs, didn't you? And how to take Communion.

If Grandma and Grandpa were Jewish, would *we* be? I said. Would we think Jesus was the savior then?

Take the other end of this sheet, she said. Help me fold it.

By the time I was in fifth grade we didn't go to church much anymore except for Christmas, maybe Easter on a good year. We were busier, I think. Sundays were for chores and homework.

That November I spent every Sunday holed up in the shed where we kept the lawnmower. I didn't let anyone in. For months I'd hoarded Styrofoam and, with the privacy afforded me in the name of science, I was finally putting all of it to use. I'd collected

Styrofoam of all types: the squeaky-snug blocks from the VCR box, the peanut variety Mom kept the Nativity set in, chunks of Mom's old swimming kickboard, a Unocal 76 antenna ball, more peanuts, these from one of Dad's FedEx boxes. Unlike the other peanuts, the FedEx variety dissolved futuristically in liquid.

I'd taken gasoline from the metal jug beside the lawnmower and measured out equal volumes into a dozen juice cups. To each cup I added a different type of Styrofoam. I'd been told this particular mixture stirred nicely into a kind of domestic napalm. Problem was, the ratio and type of Styrofoam are never specified in urban legend.

To mix my samples I used an old camping fork. I labeled the cups X-1 through X-12. X-9 contained the water-soluble Styrofoam, which congealed better than the others, forming a yellow sludge that stuck even to windows. But the real test was flammability. I lit the 12 samples like prayer candles and observed with glee that X-9 was among the best burners, similar to Sterno, and *very* difficult to put out. My data was conclusive. I extinguished Project X by shoveling dirt over it and returned to the house to wash my hands before dinner.

Ever since we rebuilt it, the house had a different feel. I'd never fully adjusted to it or felt at home there. Warm wood paneling had been replaced by formal pinstriped wallpaper. Where once there'd been a den and a fireplace there was now a cold, cavernous room with oversized windows and skylights that brought too much of the outside in. It wasn't a place to seek shelter anymore. It was a shoebox diorama.

Mom was sitting at the card table in the living room, hunched over her monthly mail-order jigsaw puzzle. It was an obsession dating to her pregnancy with me when Dad gave her the ceiling of the Sistine Chapel in 9,000 pieces. A thousand a month, he'd told her. She subdivided the pieces by color, using an entire box of zip-lock baggies: off-white pieces, bright-white pieces, yellow-white pieces, blue-white pieces. She made sure the final piece was the tip of Adam's finger touching God's. It snapped into place not before my birth, but after Todd's. Three years later.

How's the family scientist? she asked.

Starving, I said.

Dad came downstairs. It was his first week on his new job. The bank had pulled out of Nevada a few months earlier, and though Mr. Ligon offered Dad a job managing home loans at a branch in Utah—a promotion in all but the geographic sense—Todd and I cried for hours at the prospect of relocating. Life would be different (over) in Ogden. Dad had declined the offer, and the department he oversaw was soon phased out. He'd stayed with the branch as an account manager and eventually as a teller until at last the sign on the door changed. Now he sold insurance.

It wasn't his favorite job, I could tell. One time I asked what he did at work and he said people bet him they were going to get hit by a train or that their house was going to burn down. All he had to do, as I understood it, was bet against them. Like at the casinos downtown, he told me. A few lucky pessimists win their bets, but overall the house wins.

One thing hadn't changed, though. Dad still wore the gray, ball-hugging sweatpants and hooded sweatshirt Todd and I called The Outfit. Dad owned multiple, indistinguishable sets. No logos. The kind of sweats that might be issued in basic training, or prison. Dad got his at Mervyn's. He used to jog three miles each night before dinner and when I was younger I'd shadowed him on my bike. The day Todd was old enough to tag along was the day I stopped going. Eventually, Todd lost interest too and Dad decided his day job was tiresome enough. The Outfit was a remnant. It had outlived the routine.

Dad peeked into the refrigerator and began to graze.

When we going to see Frankenstein? he asked.

That's what he called my science project. And it was with each passing day more of a monster lumbering toward me. I had no idea what my project would be. I'd spent all my time fiddling with napalm recipes.

Dad poured himself a fistful of peanuts and offered me some. I accepted.

Soon, I said with my mouth full.

Looking forward to it, he said. The fair's what—next Monday?

He'll be fine, Mom said. He's been in the shed practically all afternoon.

Are you expecting any more FedEx's, Dad? I asked.

Not that I know of, he said, coaxing a few more peanuts from the can before replacing the lid. He pointed at me.

You're not using the saw, are you?

After dinner, I took a shower. The water gushed against my back, around my neck, off my nose. I liked to sit on the tiles by the drain. Mom complained these tiles didn't match the showroom samples, but I kind of liked them. Each was green but with its own texture and splotches. They were farmland viewed from a plane. I stayed crouched this way for a long time. Judging by the amount of steam, I may have even slept. The hot water supply was lukewarm by the time I got out. That night in bed I forced myself to think scientific thoughts. Perhaps I'd awake with a hypothesis. Instead, it was a congestion headache.

Mom offered little pity. She said if you go to bed with wet hair, that's what happens. She did, however, inadvertently offer me a solution. When I was younger she had subscribed me to *World* magazine, the kid-oriented offshoot of *National Geographic*. I hardly read it anymore, but vaguely recalled a cover showcasing readers' best science projects. A few minutes of rooting through the back issues in my closet proved fruitful. It was no coincidence that the data points reported in my project corroborated those gathered by Eugene, age 12, of Tuscaloosa, AL, who had poured a cupful of different brands of gasoline into an empty lawnmower, each time recording the time it took the machine to seize up. Chevron gas, we both concluded (or, in the interest of scientific integrity, I *surmised*) burned most efficiently. Sunday night before the fair I unveiled the folding poster display to my family.

Where'd you get the different gasolines? Mom asked.

Rode my bike to a bunch of gas stations, I said.

Todd was suspicious: They sold you gas?

I told them what I was doing and they donated it, I said, quoting directly from Eugene's interview.

Well, Mom said. I think it's quite a project! It's so smart of you. And you'll write each station a thank you note?

He mentions them right here, Dad said, in the Acknowledgements.

I smiled. Unocal 76 *had* provided a Styrofoam antenna ball. I felt little in the way of remorse, probably because Eugene's project struck me as straightforward. Given time, anyone could have come up with it.

My smugness lasted until I was alone in bed and I realized that if Eugene had a project worthy of nationwide publication, I could be sitting on a winner. Panic clutched my heart and squeezed. I hardly slept.

At the breakfast table the next morning, I leaned my head on my hand and fell asleep for a second. Mom poured me some Life and told me to change my shirt. I toyed with my Life, watching milk trickle from spoon to bowl. I saw my poster display being cordoned off, my hands cuffed. I didn't know where they'd take an offender like me. Maybe to wherever it was they took Rhett Cohen the time he pulled a knife on Mrs. Vee.

The green-and-white one, Mom was saying. Or the blue?

The fair was held in the multipurpose room. They made us

stand beside our projects while the judges milled about, asking questions. I answered the best I could, thinking all the while about how satisfying it would feel to fling napalm like a frenzied monkey. To stand by as flames climbed the giant stage curtain and the finger paintings on the walls curled in the heat and blown circuits sent sparks dancing across on the linoleum and the children and judges—hesitant at first to abandon their projects—were left no choice but to clog the exits in a mad dash for the playground. And no evidence would remain to prove I'd cheated on my project.

After the judging we were dismissed to recess, but I loitered near the double doors. I saw a woman with a briefcase go in, chatting with a man holding a clipboard. I felt my project to be vulnerable without me inside to guard it, to fend off the suspicious. Just before school ended they read the winners over the PA system. When 1st place was announced I sighed out of both exhaustion and elation. It wasn't me. Then the principal read my name. I'd placed 2nd. My classmates clapped for me and I took a disgraceful little bow, relieved to have been spared the added scrutiny of regional competition.

When Mom came home that afternoon I pretended to be asleep on the couch. The silver medal was already buried in my closet, behind my stack of *World* back issues. Mom dropped her keys on the counter and rushed into the family room. I don't know why I suspected she wouldn't know already. Reno is a small town. News is a brushfire.

Second place! she said.

I can see now, that had I been caught cooking napalm and faking my way through school in fifth grade, this story would have been snuffed out right about here. As it was, my fuse remained lit, doing what fuses do best: postponing the inevitable.

THREE

Mom worked puzzles whilst enjoying Sally Jesse Raphael. Likewise, she insisted Todd and I play a board game during *MacGyver* to offset the brain damage TV wreaked on our budding minds. We tried Crossbows and Catapults, a game where each player constructs a battlement from plastic bricks to defend against his opponent's rubber-band-powered medieval weaponry. The game proved too loud and interactive: we couldn't truly engage the TV. So we tried Battleship, which wasn't bad, except that in order to relay our alphanumeric torpedo strikes we had to talk over the show.

Checkers was perfect. We evolved droid-like alter-egos to play the game for us. Using merely peripheral vision and the subconscious sector of our brains we jumped and kinged one another, all the while giving practically undivided attention to the show.

Like MacGyver, Todd and I carried red Swiss Army Knives. We were always on the prowl for opportunities to jerry-rig our way out of sticky situations or simply get the better of people. Once, I taped a bunch of light bulbs to a piece of plywood and set it behind the tire of the Wagoneer. But when Dad backed out of the garage he didn't think it was a flat tire like the guys Mac duped. Dad thought I was grounded. I spent those long afternoons confined to my room, tortured by the possibility that I'd used the wrong brand of bulb.

The day Mrs. Lafleur called to tell Mom I might be a genius, Todd and I were watching the episode where MacGyver reclaims a horse stolen from a king. In Mac's voiceover, he tells us it's possibly the most expensive horse alive. He sneaks into a tent, saddles the horse and gallops away pursued by henchmen. A helicopter lowers a line, which Mac ties to the saddle, and he and the steed are lifted away. Knowing Mac's fear of heights, loyal viewers like Todd and I were all the more awed. Later on, Mac concocts a diversion bomb made from weed killer and sugar. (Kids: these aren't as easy as Mac makes them look, especially since the weed killer companies started adding flame retardant to the sodium chlorate.)

The one thing that could distract Todd from the show was a ringing phone. Since being granted the privilege of answering it, he tended to beat the rest of us there and, gathering his breath, utter the authorized greeting: Brooks residence...Todd speaking.

He listened, then cupped his hand over the receiver. Mo-om! he said. It's some lady from scho-ol!

Mom was working a new puzzle given to her on Mother's Day. Dad had found a specialty shop back east and sent them a picture of Todd and me horsing around in a pile of autumn leaves. They broke the picture into thousands of interlocking pieces. Jigsawers like Mom know leaves are among the more challenging things to reconstruct.

Put her on, Mom said, scanning the speckled oranges, yellows, and reds, her piece at the ready. She tended to talk on speakerphone to keep her hands free for puzzling. Todd pushed the button for her.

This is Anne Brooks, she said.

Yes, Mrs. Brooks. Marlene Lafleur.

I didn't know who this Mrs. Lafleur was but she seemed to know all about me. In a voice that sounded at once soothing and condescending, she explained to Mom that my 6th grade standardized test scores made me eligible for the middle school Academically Gifted program.

Todd resituated himself on the carpet, studied the board, and jumped one of my men. I retaliated by reflex.

You double-jumped yourself, dumb ass, Todd said.

But I was hanging on Mrs. Lafleur's every word. From what I gathered, my 6th grade teacher had been consulted on the matter and concurred: Oby Brooks was brilliant. While this all came as news to me, it was no surprise to Mom. The way she spoke, it was as if she'd been expecting this call ever since my gargantuan head lodged in her birth canal, necessitating a Caesarean.

I volunteer at the elementary school Tuesdays and Thursdays, Mom said. I know for a fact that AG starts in 3rd grade. How come Oby wasn't considered then? He's our resident scientist.

Many children bloom late, Mrs. Lafleur said.

And Todd? Mom asked.

I'm sorry?

My youngest. He might be smarter than Oby, actually—if you don't base it on test scores. Todd's our resident artist.

Todd set down his checkers and pushed the mute button on the television remote.

And what grade is Todd in? Mrs. Lafleur asked.

Mom looked over at Todd and me. She cocked her head to the side, taking us in, looking as though she was thinking of how best to describe a set of antique furniture to a potential buyer on the other line.

Mrs. Brooks?

Yes, sorry, Mom said. Third, now. Todd's in third. I suppose he could be in fourth, if he wanted.

Mrs. Brooks, I oversee the middle school AG program. We're in no way affiliated with the elementary school program.

Well you ought to affiliate, Mom said, scratching the tip of her nose with a puzzle piece. For a smart program, you sure are structured dumbly.

I suffered from migraines. I'd gotten my first one at Garret Moore's eleventh birthday party the year before. We'd gone to the indoor paintball place, its walls and floors slick from the grease of splattered ammo. Steam machines, strobe lights and sirens added nerve-racking realism to our skirmishes. Garret's mother bought us Mountain Dew from the snack bar to wash down the chocolate cake. Cowering for cover behind a gigantic wooden spool, I first noticed my neck was tight. Soon I saw stars. Half an hour later, I was curled on the couch in the manager's office, waiting for Mom to come pick me up and, with any luck, end me Old Yeller-style. Never before had I known such rabid, inescapable misery.

But now I had reason to suspect that migraines were the price I paid for Herculean brainpower.

Being smart would explain a lot. It would mean my quirks were actually the outlets of a pent-up intelligence. Flexing my hamstrings as streetlamps passed on car rides, yanking out armpit hair in clumps, smelling my fingers all the time—these were not behaviors I needed to keep to myself, but rather habits those with smaller brains should consider emulating. If I fart, it's art. For so long I'd been called shy. Turned out, I was pensive. My daydreams all of a sudden seemed of consequence. When Dad used to work at the bank, he had a dictaphone, but he didn't use it anymore. Maybe he'd lend it to me. I'd record nuggets of insight throughout the day and transcribe them into book form by candlelight. Illuminate posterity with my brilliance.

How would teachers grade me if my incorrect answers were actually little passive-aggressive protests? Sure, I left the answer blank: the year Columbus sailed doesn't take into account the aboriginal perspective. X=7.5? Good, fantastic—that's what the kid who used the book last year got, too, and the kid before that. Me, I'm no slave to the answer key. The answer will never change. Should we not aspire to be more than human calculators? Rise up. Rise!

I had often imagined Nazis or their equivalent storming my house in the predawn hours, holding my family at gunpoint while they quizzed me about song lyrics and firecracker model numbers, my family's lives at stake. And I always knew the answers, enunciating the oh whey oh's of "Walk Like an Egyptian" even as they pistol-whipped me.

But I hadn't taken the AG qualifying exam yet. My giftedness was only speculation. At school I found myself vibrating in my desk, mentally primed for whatever. Anything.

Mrs. Lafleur was supposed to stop in on one of my classes sometime that day. But lunch had come and gone. The afternoon was drawing to a close. Lectures seemed pointless. I found myself tuning out. What could they expect? A new clarity was mine, and my first realization was that everything at school was taught to the lowest common denominator. I'd been lifted above the maze.

I was in English class, with just over an hour to go, when a bullfrog of a woman pried open the classroom door and stuck her head in. A constellation of moles dotted her face and neck. In a whisper everyone could hear, she apologized for interrupting and winked at Mr. Sala. I laid my pencil into the crease of my book and tugged the tongues of my high-tops into readiness. Mr. Sala excused himself from the front of the class and held conference with Mrs. Lafleur in the corner. I couldn't make out what they were saying about me.

Then Mr. Sala strode up my row and huddled beside Heather Crighton, who got up, pushed in her chair, and left the room with

Mrs. Lafleur.

Heather Cry-a-ton? The one who wept just about every day and told the bus driver whenever my friends and I threw stuff out the windows? The one who struck out in kickball? The one who dipped French fries in mayo and read babysitter romances during recess?

The girl sitting in front of me turned around. Please stop, she said.

Stop what?

She pointed at my leg, twitching under her desk. Twenty minutes passed. She turned around again. I looked at my leg—at it again.

Heather came back. The discreet way she eased the classroom door shut made her all the more conspicuous. We all knew she'd been tapped. She breezed up my row, right past me, and halted at Tom's desk. She bent over and whispered something to him, then returned to her seat. As Tom rose to go, I felt my skin catching fire. I wondered whether I should go to Mrs. Lafleur's office and let her know Tom couldn't wink. Oh, and that he ate binder paper.

Tom came back for Celeste (Celeste!). Celeste left, then returned to tap Jeremy, who seemed angry about the interruption to his work. Upon his return, Jeremy forsook tradition. He did not tiptoe. He did not whisper.

Oby! he blurted.

I hustled to the office, afraid school would let out and forfeit my eligibility. Mrs. Lafleur met me there and shook my hand. She ushered me into a large supply closet. There were reams and reams of binder paper stacked along the walls. I wondered whether Tom had managed to abstain during his visit here.

Please, she said, waving an upturned palm over a small table with nothing on it. There were two chairs, identical.

Where do I sit? I asked.

You pick.

Aha! So the depth-sounding of my wits had begun. I took the chair closest to the door—the one MacGyver would pick. Mrs. Lafleur asked me to comment on a picture of an African tribeswoman and identify congruent triangles. A bare light bulb lent our interview the feel of an interrogation. She read me questions from a booklet. I remember one in particular:

Bo is both the 50th best and 50th worst student at his school. How many students attend Bo's school?

A hundred students, I answered right away. No—wait.

The answer didn't feel right. I furrowed my brow and looked around for inspiration. I looked at the paper on the shelves. Each stack was nine packages high. The 5th highest pack was also the 5th lowest pack, with four packages above and below it.

It's 99, I said.

This answer seemed to please Mrs. Lafleur.

Hey, Bo—whoever you are—you would have guessed 100, which is why you're stuck forever in the fattest part of the bell curve, you mediocre piece of shit.

FOUR

AG class convened Thursdays at an elementary school near the airport. We took a bus, picking up fellow dorks from other schools along the way. The first day, we arrived at the host school during recess. Soccer seemed to predominate. As agile with their feet as their hands, kids were playing soccer with volleyballs and basketballs and kickballs. They went scuttling across the crusty sand of the baseball infield and juggled in nebulous circles on the asphalt four-square courts. Others hung from jungle gyms, staring at us as we walked to our classroom. We were lanky middle schoolers with big ears and freckles, a herd of giraffes stepping gingerly among monkeys.

Heather, Tom, Celeste, and I had made the cut. Rumor was, Jeremy had been selected, too, only to turn it down. I think that Jeremy, arguably the brightest of us all, regarded his smarts as a handicap. A big brain didn't impress the dudes he hung with. It didn't impress my dudes much either, but it sure impressed Mom. As for Dad, well, when he learned of my AG status he let the newspaper go limp in his hands so he could look at me across the breakfast table, wink, and pull the pages taut again. Each of my accomplishments was a chapter in Dad's favorite book, the one he'd read so many times that there were no longer plot twists, just expectations.

How much is it? he'd asked.

Oh for Christ's sake, Stan, Mom yelled from the laundry room. AG is a district program!

Dad winked to me again, but kept his voice gruff. We still pay for it with taxes, honey! Even the stupid families pay for AG.

We waited together, Dad and I, listening to the sounds in the laundry room. I started to laugh, but he shushed me with a finger to his lips.

Well maybe, Mom yelled, Oby ought to write those families thank you notes.

That night we went out to dinner and I got to choose where we went, though they must have known I'd choose Sizzler. From our table we could see through a door into the kitchen. Two cooks worked diligently, taming flame-ups, halving onions. Todd and I capped our straws with our fingers and lifted suctioned 7Up to our mouths, over and over and over again.

They know how to make so many things, I said.

Who? Mom asked.

I pointed to the cooks.

Oh, Dad said. Well, they've got recipes.

I like recipes. Maybe I'll be a cook.

No, you won't.

<hr>

There are all kinds of smart kids. There's the hand-up-for-every-question kind, who will grow up a lawyer or a doctor, but no matter what, will become an asshole. There's the math specialist. The book worm. There's the albino introvert who smirks at everything you say and will one day crash a halftime show to protest an obscure tariff. But smart is relative. And so, despite prevailing archetypes, our little clan of whiz kids took on new roles. At our own schools we stood out as geeks and kiss-ups, whereas at AG we became homogeneous. This couldn't last. Soon, we had a resident kiss-up of the kiss-ups, a bully, a freak, even a bunch of average Joes. Filler. Kids who swam all the strokes, though not very elegantly. Do you remember Otis Birdsong? Few do. The year I started going to AG, Otis was on the same NBA All-Star team as Kareem and Magic.

The classroom we used varied. Papier-mâché U.S. presidents dangled from the ceiling one week, and the next we'd find ourselves staring at a conga line of alphabetically organized animals. Our mentor changed just as often. The first week it was a towering black man with freckled bags under his eyes and gapped teeth. He went to the back of the class and aimed the longest finger I'd ever seen at a map of the world.

Name this country, he said. His accent, to my surprise, was British.

Africa, someone blurted.

The benefit of the doubt: the map was both physical and political, with mountain ranges and river systems obscuring borders. And the man's finger was so long it seemed incapable of indicating anything less than a continent.

Turns out, I'd said it. I think I was set up. When the lawyers in the front of the class turned to glare, I felt like turning around, too, to object to myself. I hadn't realized it quite yet, but it wouldn't be long: I was the Otis Birdsong of AG.

We were treated to all kinds of interesting lectures from all kinds of interesting people. A Buddhist came once. He had a sun-bleached pony tail, tinted glasses, and teeth that were similar in hue to the tea he drank throughout the day. He told us that in Tibet the word for life is *sok*, and that to have *sok* means two things: giving off heat and having consciousness. This might have been more interesting if I wasn't so distracted by the unexplained presence of a 10-speed bike near the coat rack. I later learned that the bike was the Buddhist's. After class he strapped his bag to the handlebars and rode off across the playground. It was weird for some reason, seeing a teacher on a bike.

A doctor came and told us about genetics. He said that I have 200 genes in common with every living thing on Earth—donkeys, mushrooms, Bell Curve Bo, Heather Crighton—and that most of who I am was decided before I was even born.

What about what I'm going to do? I asked.

Sure, he said. To some extent. Do you like chocolate?

I guess.

Take it or leave it, huh? he said. I'd say that puts you in Category Number One. Category Number Two being people who love it, and Category Number Three being the addicted. I'm a Three.

At this, the doctor patted his formidable paunch.

Is this just random? he continued. Was my mother eating Hershey bars while she breastfed me? Or did my DNA dictate that I would have just the right ratio of sweet and bitter taste buds and extra chocoholic neurons in my brain? It's probably all of the above. So when I decide to buy chocolate instead of carrots and I get fat, my DNA is at least somewhat to blame. It's had a hand in sealing my fate.

This prompted me to wonder about the future coded into my own chromosomes. How could I be blamed for anything ever again when I wasn't even in charge of myself?

Then there was Dr. Watanabe, a professor of Japanese from the university. She wore pleated khakis and a black T-shirt. Her wiry black mane was interspersed with grey and fell halfway down her back. She gave us a lesson writing Japanese characters with calligraphy brushes.

How can anybody read this? someone asked, and we all laughed. (It wasn't me who asked.)

They learn when they're kids, Dr. Watanabe said. Just like you learn English. If you'd been born in Japan, you'd know how to read it.

I studied the characters, imagining what it would feel like to know their meanings without thinking. Then she showed us how to fold paper into pterodactyls. Cranes, she called them.

In Japan, she said, it's believed that if you fold a thousand cranes, your heart's desire will come true.

She told the story of a girl who'd been exposed to radiation during the bombing of Hiroshima and later developed leukemia. To defeat her cancer the girl started folding. 644—that's how many she finished. They buried her with a wreath made from the birds, including 356 folded by diligent classmates. Dr. Watanabe passed around a picture of the Hiroshima Peace Park. There's a sculpture of the girl there, a crane perched to fly from her fingertips.

If you'd like, Dr. Watanabe said, we can all fold cranes and I'll put them in a big box and send them to Hiroshima. They get cranes every day from kids like you all over the world.

So she passed around square paper and we started folding for peace. She showed us a slideshow of the mushroom cloud and of people's shadows tattooed on sidewalks and their burn scars. She told us as much as she knew about uranium and nuclear fission.

That night, Hiroshima left its tiny scar on me—an arc of darkened skin on my thumb, near the halfway joint. I was chopping celery C's for Mom's salad, the knife snapping rhythmically through the stringy stalks. Dad came home from work and helped himself to bourbon. Todd was setting the kitchen table. Mom was washing something in the sink. I, momentarily, was at 31,600 feet, looking down from a B-29 Superfortress. Dr. Watanabe told us that when the 10,000-pound bomb detached and plummeted away, the plane, suddenly much lighter, jumped a little. Forty-three seconds later the sky went yellow, then pink. The plane's wings quivered as though made of paper.

Oby, Mom said. For Christ's sake.

Mm?

You're bleeding all over the celery!

I went to the bathroom to find a Band-Aid and ended up popping zits. It wasn't that I wanted to kill anybody, or that I was blind to human suffering. I was suffering. I was thirteen. That night, Mom found me asleep on the carpet in my room, my clothes and shoes still on.

This is becoming a habit, she said.

So? I said.

I liked being asleep. I was always yearning to fall asleep. I was Category Number Three for sleep. Sleep was just about the only time I didn't have to pretend anything. My body was embroiled in a revolution. It festered bubbles of puss on my neck. It sprouted dark hair that itched. Or, I'd wake up in the morning overcome with unexpected shame, the feel of someone else's skin still lingering against my own, a sticky spot on my comforter. It didn't even fit me anymore, this body. Often it reeked. My soul was a hermit crab, inhabiting a loaner bowling shoe.

I look back. I see myself being driven somewhere in the back-seat of a wood-paneled Wagoneer. I see posters of Lamborghinis, cars about which I still know next to nothing other than that they're maybe Italian and they're expensive so the doors open funny and they're not Wagoneers. I see Mossimo and Stüssy and Quicksilver. Nike Airs and Reebok Pumps.

I didn't want to kill anybody. I would have folded cranes until my cuticles were a bloody lattice if it meant for once I could just be noticed, just go off, and at the same time obliterate all evidence of my ever existing. I wanted to shake the fucking globe. I wanted to hide in the corner. I wanted to get it over with, everything over with.

Remember what they named that pent-up barrel of uranium, the one they dropped on Hiroshima? Little Boy.

FIVE

M r. Weisgard wore safety goggles, a lab coat, and rubberized gloves so thickly reinforced he could have thrown lava balls. We filed up the rows of desks and settled into our seats. At the front table, blue cones of flame tickled the undersides of beakers. Mr. Weisgard was making adjustments to a tall metal tube. He was the type of teacher who need not call the class to attention. He just *waited*. He spoke not a word. Eventually, Heather realized we were all looking at her, but Mr. Weisgard waited a little longer. Then his deep voice took command of the silence.

Any of you AG whiz kids ever cook at home? he asked.

The usual hands shot up.

Good, he said. So what's the difference between cooking and chemistry? Put your hands down. I'm gonna tell you. The difference is, there is no difference.

Mr. Weisgard had himself quite an Adam's apple. His black mustache and impossibly white teeth reminded me of the Marlboro man, and when he stepped out from behind his bubbling apparatus I saw his dusty rancher's boots, with raised heels and a flap of fringe at the toe. I couldn't shake a feeling that I'd seen him before.

The AG folks have been begging me to come teach you guys for years, he said, jabbing a knife into a sack of flour. I teach chemistry at the high school down the road, juniors and seniors mostly, but they assured me you're all very mature and that you've got good noodles, so I figured you could handle a lecture on rapid oxidation.

Had I heard right? I inched forward in my seat and looked around, needing to confirm with my classmates that, indeed, I had reason to be pleasantly flabbergasted. But my searching eyes met with blank stares. From Mr. Weisgard's vantage point I must have looked like the first popcorn kernel in the pan to jiggle.

Oby, he said, reading my origami name card. The heck kind of name is that?

Oh. It's Toby really. My brother couldn't say the T when he was little. Strange thing is, his name is Todd.

Odd, said Mr. Weisgard.

Yeah, I said. But, no. We call him Todd.

I see. Well, you looked like you were about to oxidize there, son. Spontaneously! Do you need to visit the little boy's room or would you rather tell us what I'm talking about?

I'm not sure, I said.

Oh. All right. I'll ask someone who knows.

He looked the class over for a volunteer, pulling off his safety goggles to show just how patient he was willing to be. I couldn't take it.

It's an explosion, I said.

Sorry?

I raised my voice a notch: *An explosion.*

Whoo-eee! he hollered. He put his goggles back on and tossed me a pair of my own. I'd earned an assistantship.

Come on up here, son, he said.

He spooned some flour into a little pile on a piece of wax paper and issued me a sifter. I started sifting.

Now we're cooking, he said, and turned to the class. Do any of you ever make S'mores? It's hard to keep your marshmallow from catching fire, isn't it? Okay—why are you raising your hands? I'm beginning to think some of you don't know what a rhetorical question is. Mr. Egan, why exactly is your hand up?

I thought you were asking us what a rhetorical question was.

Instead, how about you tell us what marshmallows are made of.

Eggs?

I'm impressed, Mr. Egan. Egg whites, to be specific. Anything else?

Sugar?

Indeed! Sugar. And because they're full of sugar and sugar's full of energy, marshmallows burn like the dickens when you toss them in a campfire. He put his hand on my back and peeked over my shoulder to see how my sifting was coming along. I was on at least my fifth iteration.

That's enough, he said.

He pried the sifter from my hands. If left unchecked I'd happily have sifted Mr. Weisgard's flour to atomic fineness.

Flour is a carbohydrate, he told the class. Therefore, what Mr. Oby here has just done is to sift us the equivalent of a pile of microscopic marshmallows.

He tore himself a square of tinfoil and folded a crease down the middle, into which he poured about half the flour. He set a Bunsen burner on the floor. The metal tube I'd noticed earlier was open at both ends. He set one end down over the burner, routing the burner's gas hose through a small notch cut in the side of the tube; this created a chimney almost as tall as I was, with a flame in its belly. I was told to return to my desk.

Mr. Weisgard tilted the flour into the top of the tube. An instant later there was a gentle '*whoomp*' and the chimney blew some fire.

Don't you love that? he asked. Suddenly wary of responding to questions, many of us just smiled. None of us had blinked for at least a minute. We've got more flour, he said. Let's do it again.

I think it was the burly mischievousness of Mr. Weisgard's voice that suddenly reminded me who he was, at least who he was to the Boy Scouts at Glacial Meadows two summers before. He was a member of the mountain man brigade, an elite trio of bearded badasses who even at chapel never took off their hunting frocks, fringed leather pants and possum caps. They carried tomahawks and had their own campsites in the Rendezvous Corral. Our troop got to spend an afternoon in there. I remember throwing a few 'hawks, a few knives. Savage weapons, I'd realized, the instant I heard the deafening report of a muzzleloader.

AG had been dismissed to lunch and I was alone in the classroom. I leaned my head over the barrel of the flour-burning chimney and gazed down, just to see.

Careful there, said Mr. Weisgard. He was standing in the doorway.

Startled, I stepped away and apologized.

No, no, said Mr. Weisgard. It's fine.

He went to his desk, sat down, and ripped into a piece of beef jerky. I went to my backpack, grabbed my lunch and turned to go, but I couldn't help myself.

I think I know you from Scout camp, I said.

He looked up, chewing.

The older guys in my troop shot black powder rifles with you, I added.

Yeah?

His voice rose an octave. He fidgeted with a beaker stand that

didn't seem to demand attention. I felt as though I'd caught a su-
perhero at his day job. He asked my rank.

Star, I said.

Hang in there. It's worth it.

I'll try, I said. Are you an Eagle Scout?

He tore off another hunk of jerky and chewed on it for a while.
Afraid not, he said.

I think he was about to add something but I accidentally interrupted: What are we doing after lunch break?

His brow furled. I'm gonna let it be a surprise, he said. But do
me a favor. Pilfer me some salt from the cafeteria.

A pill of salt?

Pilfer. Filch, pinch, lift—what do you AG kids say?

What?

He stood up, took me by the shoulders, and stared me in the
eye. I could smell musky cologne and possibly wood smoke.

Mr. Oby, he said. This is a direct order. Steal me some salt.
From the cafeteria. We'll use it in the demonstration this afternoon.

I think the salt is free.

All the better! I seem to recall something about honesty in the
Scout Law.

No, I said, just trustworthiness.

He studied me for a moment. Oby, he said, do you know who
Gandhi was?

I guess so.

Yeah, well, Gandhi, he lived in India, and one time he walked
for twenty-three days just to get to the ocean and pick up a single
grain of salt. All I'm asking you to do is get me a packet or two.
From the lunchroom.

I understand, Mr. Weisgard.

That's wonderful.

He started laughing and we shared something for a moment—something like kinship. Perhaps it was scouting or maybe a common love of rapid oxidation, but we weren't so different, he and I. In fact, the twinkle of approval in Mr. Weisgard's eye when he coerced me into stealing sodium chloride was all I needed to rationalize stealing a little back from him (minus the chloride) later that afternoon. It seemed as though he'd practically *told* me to do it, in not so many fancy words. It happened like this:

He handed out stoichiometry worksheets after lunch, further proof Mr. Weisgard was like me: he, too, postponed the inevitable. While we crunched the mathematical ratios, he flipped open a metal briefcase and pulled out a glass canister. Inside the thick glass I saw a wheel of brie. It wasn't brie, of course, but that's what it looked like. He pushed on some sort of pressure seal and pulled loose the lid. With his heavy gloves back on he took out the brie. He crammed a chisel into it, using all his weight. The inside of the brie wasn't white like the outside; it had the silvery luster of metal. He pried off a chunk about the size of his thumb, which he further divided into thirds—keeping one and putting the rest back in the canister.

Finish up the worksheets, he said. Let's go outside. Oby, bring the sodium chloride.

And so, it was that seventeen academically gifted seventh graders and a mountain man came to convene on the hard-baked infield dirt of an elementary school playground near the airport. Mr. Weisgard stood at home plate with a beaker of water. We spread out along the backstop. He tore open one of the salt packets and poured the contents into his palm. We saw the salt with new eyes, new knowledge, the way I saw girls after sex ed.

He raised his voice over the roar of a plane.

Were it not for an atom called chlorine, he said, this would be much livelier stuff to sprinkle in your soup! As we learned on the chalkboard, the other type of atom in salt is sodium.

He put on his glove and took out the chunk of soft sodium metal.

Someone please remind me, he said, what is this white film on...

We answered: So-sodi-so-um-ium-sod-oxide!-sodium-ide-hy--um-drox-ox-ide! -odi-um-drox-hydrox-sodi-ide!

Thank you all, he said. Yes. Because of the water in the air, sodium hydroxide. As you can see, we've got some water here.

We most certainly did, Mr. Weisgard. And we'd done the math.

$$2Na + 2H_2O \rightarrow 2NaOH + H_2$$

Water's chemical formula everyone knows—but not H_2O's little secret. If priests knew the hellfire pent up in water, they'd think twice about dipping babies in it. Mr. Weisgard coaxed the demons from our water. He dropped the sodium chunk in the beaker. It fizzled with ten times the voraciousness of Alka-Seltzer, staining the water blood red like some kind of exorcism. The hydrogen which had until that moment clung passively to the oxygen—well, with all that free heat and energy around for the taking, that H_2 burned like the dickens.

Later that afternoon Mr. Weisgard said we'd done enough chemistry for one day and so invited the class to the playground to join the local kids for a pick-up soccer game. Most of us stood on the sidelines instead, cheering on our guru as the clamoring munchkins swarmed, latching onto his legs, slide-tackling his ankles. No one noticed when I slipped away.

The metal briefcase was open on the table at the head of the classroom. I cut myself a wedge of brie and put it in a sandwich baggie I'd saved from lunch, taking care to squeeze all the extra air out before I sealed the zip lock.

Mr. Weisgard: you were right. Chemistry *can* feel a lot like cooking.

SIX

Kelly Atkinson was my friend by proximity. He lived on Dartmouth, three houses up, so we shared a bus stop. Our paths rarely crossed during school, but he had a knack for getting himself invited over in the afternoons. With two older sisters, he tended to avoid his own house.

Mom kept the pantry stocked with little cans of Vienna sausage just for Kelly. He'd arrange the sausage in pyramids on a square of paper towel in the microwave, then nibble away while we played Nintendo. Mrs. Atkinson said video games gave kids a false sense of reality. She didn't allow Nintendo at Kelly's house. We didn't tell my mom that. She limited our video game time as it was, which made Kelly's mastery of Nintendo frustrating: for Kelly, a single turn on Super Mario Brothers could last half an hour, minutes Mom counted against my daily allocation.

Sometimes Kelly convinced me to rearrange my room. Though I feigned reluctance, I liked waking up the next morning in a different corner, facing different posters. It felt grown up: I'd rented a new apartment. Kelly's penchant for redecorating and his collection of mint-condition Transformers, and probably his wavy hair, left my friends no choice but to write him off as a, quote-unquote, fag. I knew him to be more of a barnacle.

On the day I smuggled sodium home in my backpack, Kelly clung. It was the day before Halloween, which was a school holiday that year since it fell on the same day as Nevada Day. The AG bus had returned me to school with a little time left before the final bell. I heard music escaping from the Halloween dance in the lunchroom and considered stopping in, but the dance was toward the end, which meant all the songs would be slow songs and the mere thought of latching my clammy self onto a girl for three-and-a-half minutes of asynchronous swaying, perfumed perspiration and darting eyes, the bubbling feeling in my guts—well, it was all so risky. So uncontrollable.

I visited my locker and went back out to the turnaround to get on yet another bus. I retreated to the back and sat down. The driver kept her eye on me in her big, bubbled mirror. I slouched down enough that the seat in front of me shielded me from her purview.

The sun was already low against the mountains, exaggerating the shadows, providing little heat. I saw myself reflected in the window. Whenever I caught a glimpse of my face, I couldn't help picking at it, sometimes attacking fresh zits and drawing blood. Students poured from the school in a joyous evacuation before the three-day weekend. Most of their costumes had hardly survived the day, or had been reapportioned. Doctors carried sickles, vampires sported clown afros. I was among the only ones on the bus not dressed up. The oozing sores on my forehead were real.

And I was starving. Maybe I needed some candy to pull my blood sugar level out of its nosedive. Candy is not hard to come by at a public middle school the day before Halloween, but I lacked so much as a Nerd pebble—a fact hinting at the widening fissure between them and me.

Leaving school for AG once a week meant I was constantly playing catch-up on rumors and mischief. Middle school society was a game of crack the whip, and I clung one-handed at the mercy of the tail end. None of my friends took the bus anymore, so the ride home was a lonely commute. I could have sat by Kelly, but that would only have encouraged him. And it rarely mattered in the end: we still got off the bus together, an unhappy married couple bound by routine and real estate.

Mom called soon after we got to the house. She was at a Junior League meeting and wouldn't be home for another hour. While Kelly stacked sausage, I snagged a pair of rubber gloves from under the kitchen sink. He looked like he was about to ask me what I was doing.

Shut up, I said.

The gloves were damp, so I made Kelly hold Mom's hairdryer while I rubbed and clapped my hands in front of it. I wasn't taking chances. Todd came home from school and followed the noise into my parents' bathroom.

What the hell? he said.

Don't worry about it, Kelly said, waving the dryer up and down my palms.

Todd brushed Kelly off. He looked at me: What're you doing, Oby?

Nothing. And you can't watch.

You two are going to hump.

Fuck off.

Are you going to blow something up?

I said fuck off.

You're going to blow something up.

I pinned him to the carpet and he kicked me in the thigh. I grabbed his hair with my rubber gloves and bashed his head into the floor. We wrestled around until we were breathing hard, and then I got up. He walked off but I continued to feel his eyes lurking behind furniture, through shuttered blinds.

We see you, Todd, I said. Stop acting like an idiot.

Seriously, added Kelly.

Whatever, girl's name, Todd replied.

Just shut up, I said. Both of you!

The tendons in the back of my neck were bridge cables. My eyeballs thumped in time with my quickening heart. A bead of sweat ran from my armpit down my side. As with a hurricane, warning signs portend the arrival of a migraine. And yet, somehow, when the levees finally burst and the waters pound their way in, it still comes as a surprise.

I didn't need Todd and Kelly around. I wasn't putting on a show. They asked questions about everything, but it wasn't the stoichiometry they cared for. So I just stopped trying to explain and kept quiet while I pried free a chunk of the sodium with one of Dad's flathead screwdrivers. Todd leaned in for a closer look. Perhaps a genetic commonality magnetized my brother to the unstable metal. I can't say. Kelly took a half-step back.

They tailed me into the backyard. When I tossed the small chunk into the pond it skated across the surface, trailing a foamy wake. The water was too murky to tell if it was turning red. Before the sodium reached the middle—but not before inciting the territorial aggression of our resident swan—the chunk sizzled to a halt and vanished.

Nice! Todd said.

Kelly agreed: Throw in a bigger one.

Yeah. Do the rest all at once.

I groaned in reply. My headache was no longer ignorable. I went inside. I suddenly wanted nothing more than to be in my room on my bed with all the lights off and the blinds shut. So that's where I went.

Kelly followed. He took a glass paperweight off my bookshelf and looked around at the furniture. I think it's better, he said, when your desk is in that corner.

I think it's better when you aren't in my room, I mumbled.

He set the paperweight down. I groaned again, for dramatic effect.

You going to leave this stuff on your desk? he said. Shouldn't we hide it or something?

We? I said. It isn't yours, Kelly. Just like this isn't your room.

I pulled a pillow over my head. Still I could hear him call me an asshole, his retreating footsteps down the hallway, and the door slam on his way out.

See you Monday, I mumbled.

Todd was pouting in his room, but he left me alone. I kept my pillows in rotation, holding whichever was coolest against my face. I knew by this point that it was a migraine, and I thought I might outsmart it by falling asleep before it seized control.

The throbbing intensified. Expanded. Only Mom's pity could soften the pain, and she wasn't home. Everything I tried brought only pain. I hated everything I lay eyes on. I hated Lamborghinis with their doors like insect wings and I hated the multitalented Bo Jackson. I saw staircases on ceilings, fish transmogrified into birds, dismembered hands sketching self-portraits. I loathed M.C. Escher.

Mom, I whispered to the dark. Mom, please. Please please please please. Mom? Please.

I curled up and whimpered, tasting a tear. I kept checking the time. The indigo numbers on my clock radio were too bright, too bright, and Mom was so late. I clutched my head and it felt like a beating heart. I remembered the sodium. I'd left it out on my desk! But when I looked it wasn't there: Kelly must have stashed it when he came in—or maybe he'd taken it. I didn't care about anything except the coldest parts of my pillows.

My eyes shut. I lost track of time.

There came a pinch at my toes.

That bad, huh pal?

Dad brushed back my dampened bangs and held his palm to my forehead. I could tell by his touch he believed in my pain. Dad was a migraine sufferer himself. I wanted to show him I could bear grownup levels of agony. I wanted to earn his empathy. We both knew that all he could give me was aspirin, water, and silence.

Mom came home soon after. I rolled over to find her crouched beside my bed. Her purse was still slung over her shoulder. She rested her hand on me.

Another one, honey?

I nodded and sniffled, wincing at the pressure added to my sinuses, aching to know how long something so crowded and throbbing could stay pent up. There was no more room in me.

Later, I listened to Mom, Dad, and Todd eating dinner. They spoke in low voices, which only made it worse for me since I had to strain to tune in to their conversation. Eavesdropping was the only diversion I could handle. I listened a little to Peter Jennings' calming voice in the family room. I started to get an appetite but couldn't convince my body it was worth getting up. The tiny summoning bell Mom had left me was too loud for its own good.

I sensed a figure in my room. Soon another. I was half-awake. The room was dark and warm and I was on my side, against the wall. I drifted off again.

Then there was a light. It swept through the room, probing, its beam a low-battery orange. A few times it shined on my side of the room but it seemed to dwell on the other. I was almost awake but didn't roll over. I felt like part of a crime scene. Suddenly my closet door slid on its track. There was a gasp.

It was Mom.

Then Dad. He swore.

I rolled over to see Mom's silhouette in the doorway, her hands on her face. Dad grabbed a pair of my jeans off the floor and started swinging them at something in my closet, as if trying to fend off a rabid animal. My shoebox of baseball cards was on fire. On the shelf below the shoebox was a stack of *World* magazines, also smoldering. I noticed one issue near the middle of the stack had something lodged inside its pages, pulsing with an intense red color too bright to look at directly. I sat up in bed. Mom was coughing. That's when I first smelled smoke and looked up to see a thin black cloud pooling against my ceiling. There was more smoke than fire. The flashlight fell to the floor and rolled to a stop with its beam directed out the window and into the cloudy night, summoning superheroes.

The fire climbed steadily. It nibbled on my baseball cards, then started on papers and old craft projects on the top shelf. The flames were young still, eating quietly. The smoke detector chirped to life, was silent for a moment, and then let out an uninterrupted and piercing screech.

God damn it! Dad said. He grabbed the glass of water off my nightstand.

Dad, I said, wait…

He didn't hesitate, using the full glass to try and douse the flames.The magazines soaked up the water, turned soggy, and smoked. As the fire subsided he dropped the empty glass and turned to look at me. It wasn't anger in his eyes, nor fear. It was bewilderment. Behind him, I saw the sodium burn with new energy. It started sizzling. Dad turned to look just as brilliant white sparks showered the room. He cowered as the sparks peppered his back, some bouncing away, others clinging to his shirt. He cried out. Red bits of sodium blasted through my closet. Like shrapnel, they whizzed across the room and embedded into walls. Posters caught fire.

I'd squirreled secrets all over my closet. A box big enough to hold it all would have aroused Mom's suspicion when she came weekly to fetch my dirty clothes. So, there was an M80 or two in my church socks and batches of Styrofoam napalm in racquetball cans. An old box of markers held a dozen empty paintball CO_2 cartridges I'd filled with gunpowder and kerosene and topped off with segments of cannon fuse from the army surplus store.

The fire found things I'd forgotten. It found everything.

$2H_2O+2Na+6$TijuanaTremor$+3M80+1M90+X9+60$Black-Cat$+7$Romancandle$+24$bottlerocket$+12CO_2$grenade$+1$papier-mâché$+6$Quicksilver$+5$Stüssy$+1$OceanPacific$+500$StrikeAnywhere$+1$paint$+3$crane$+5$binder$+1$racket$+3$jean$+1$compass$+2$PinewoodDerby$+36$*WorldMagazine*$+2$trophy$+2$Nike$+1$SwissArmy$+4$Styrofoam$+1$journal$+2$cord$+19$book$+3$poster$+1$mitt$+4$lovenote$+1$hatenote$+1$Crossbow&Catapult$+1$spunksock$+1$sciencefairmedal(Ag)$+2$tape$+5$seashell$+1$Bible$+1$Sterno$+15$cassette$+13$CD$+4$belt$+2$dictionary$+1$camera$+6$iron$+3$wood$+4$Titleist$+14$shoe$+2$blanket$+1$*Penthouse*$+2$*Garfield*$+9$meritbadge$+3$frame$+2$ticket$+1$backpack$+1$footlocker$+4$pencil$+2$jacket$+8$hat$+1$Bic$+1$remotecontrol$+3$battery$+3$album$+2$bungee$+130$dollar$+45$cent$+1$Walkman$+1$BoyScoutHandbook$+1$Starburst$+1$carpet$+6$shelf$+4$wall$+1$roof$+1525$MooreDrive

Dad coughed and shouted to Todd, who'd poked his head around Mom in the doorway.

You get back! Dad said. All of you! Back!

I was using my bedspread like a flak jacket. He yanked it away.

Oby, now! he shouted. Call the fire department!

I could already feel heat from across the room and leapt for the doorway. Dad grabbed a fire extinguisher from the hall closet and pulled the pin, only to retreat as bottle rockets began hissing across the room and lodging into posters. A pair of cherry bombs exploded almost simultaneously, startling Mom into hysterics. She crumpled to her knees in the hallway and covered her ears.

What's happening? she asked, searching my eyes for an explanation. What's happening, Oby?

I said now! Dad yelled. A burning squib corkscrewed along the floor and disappeared under my nightstand. Bangers banged at random: Bang! Bang, bang! Bang, bang, bang! Bang! Upon bursting, a single banger releases five kilojoules of energy and forms a pocket of overpressure, making waves that propagate through the air at the speed of sound. Bang! Bang, bang! One hundred and sixty decibels, unless the factory worker responsible felt frisky and added an extra pinch of aluminum.

C'mon, Mom, I said. Get up. I put my hand on her back. She was shaking.

Anne, please! Dad said. Take the boys. You can't stay here.

Neither can you, Stan!

I'm right behind you!

We're not leaving Dad, are we? Todd asked, his question punctuated by a cherry bomb.

Damn it! I'll be fine, Todd. Oby, get everyone out! Take your brother and your mom and call 911! Do you understand?

Todd and I took Mom's hands and she got to her feet and let us lead her down the hallway, but she slipped away from us and ducked into her bedroom. She stood frozen at the foot of the bed, turning in all directions, scanning the room. Todd told her to hurry.

Grab something, she said.

Like what? Todd asked.

Anything!

I grabbed the cordless phone. Todd grabbed a giant glass peach from the nightstand. Mom rushed out of the room. We rejoined her in the hallway. She studied us with our things.

Yes, she said. Oby, take that stuff outside.

We need to get out, Mom. Now.

Todd handed me his peach.

We'll be right there, Mom said. Go!

I shook my head. The night air was cool when I stepped through the backdoor. Being outside at that moment was like being underwater at a pool, suddenly insulated from all the clamoring and splashing. I paused on the back patio, but only for a moment. When I came back inside, Mom and Todd were in the family room, lifting the enormous, framed Sistine Chapel off its nail. Already the house was filling with smoke.

You carry this one! she told me, leaning it against the couch. Todd and I will get the others.

Not now, Mom…

Don't you argue with me, young man.

It's too big, I said.

Then drag it!

The puzzle of Todd and me playing in the leaves was still on the table. So far she'd managed to put together most of a wheel-barrow in the background of the picture, and quite a bit of Todd's overalls. The Oby-shaded pieces were arrayed in piles around the edges of the table—flecks of blue that would be my eyes, yellows and browns that would be hair.

Mom put her hands on her mouth and stared at it, then dashed into the kitchen. When she came back she had a roll of plastic wrap. She mummified the tabletop with it, pinning down the loose pieces. Todd and I watched, somewhat impressed. She was breathing hard.

When she was done I helped her tilt the table on its edge and carry it through the kitchen door into the backyard.

The moon had ducked behind a cloud, darkening everything. From outside the house the only indication of a problem was a flickering orange light in my room and Dad's muffled cursing. We huddled together. Tiny waves on the pond lapped at the shore.

Oby Brooks, Mom said. What in God's name have you done?

I pretended not to hear her and called 911. The operator came on the line after one ring. 1525 Moore Drive is on fire, I told her, my voice much calmer than I'd expected.

Is everyone out of the house? she asked.

Not yet.

Stay put and remain on the line.

And so I stood there barefoot in the cold grass, wearing a T-shirt and boxers. My nervous hands had no pockets in which to take shelter. The adrenaline high subsided, leaving only the thump-pumping of my migraine.

I'm going back in, I muttered.

You most certainly are not, Mom said. Dad will come out when he needs to, and we're gonna be right here waiting for him.

It's my room.

What were you hiding in that closet? Do you realize how un-safe—I could just strangle you right now! And now your poor father's in there...

Is he coming out? Todd asked.

Of course, honey.

When?

A rush of wind rearranged the leaves on the patio and scat-tered new ones from the trees. I had nothing to say. I hadn't eaten since lunch, when I'd stolen the salt for Mr. Weisgard. That felt like a week ago. I hugged myself but couldn't warm up. My head pounded and stopped, pounded and stopped. Todd looked up at me as though I were a stranger. His eyes were wet and imploring. We heard the rising wail of a siren, soon joined by another. Neighborhood dogs howled.

Dad burst out the back door and sat down on the grass, coughing. He had one of my T-shirts tied over his mouth and nose. We ran over but he was up again before we reached him. Still fighting back the coughs, he let Mom hug him.

Did you put it out, Dad? Todd asked.

Dad didn't answer. He stared briefly at the mummified table, although he didn't seem to fully register it.

Oby, he said, fetch me the hose.

He detached himself from Mom's embrace and went to the side of the house and looked in my window.

Dad, I said, it was sodium. That thing in my closet. You can't put more water on it.

Dad turned to face me. I mistook the baffled look on his face for curiosity.

Water only makes it burn, I explained.

I can handle burn, Oby, he said, jabbing his finger in my chest. It's the goddamn explosions I'm having trouble with! That closet of yours—it's like a munitions locker. How dare you bring all that shit into our house! Todd, did you know about any of this? I know Mom and I sure didn't.

Some of it, Todd said.

Unbelievable! Dad said. He let go of my shoulders. Un-be-lievable.

Todd, go stand in the driveway, Mom said. Wait for the fire department and let them know we're back here.

Dad looked at me, shook his head and retied my shirt over his mouth. The Nike swoosh formed a mustache. Get me that hose, he said.

I dashed across the yard, lifted the spigot to full blast, and lugged the hose back. Dad loosened a brick from a retaining wall and threw it through my window. He picked up the metal bar we used to adjust underground sprinkler valves and knocked out the rest of the glass. Black smoke billowed out the window for a moment, then sucked back. We could feel the air rushing in.

I think you made a draft, I said.

Oh, did I? And I suppose you know a better way, smart guy?

The hose dangled limply in my hands, making mud at my feet. I handed it over. Dad said thanks. It wasn't the curt thanks he always used to acknowledge the proper completion of a duty. He over-said it, as if I'd done him a huge favor, meanwhile holding his thumb over the outlet of the hose to make it spray further. The water vanished into the dark, churning smoke inside. Through the open garage door I saw firemen jogging toward the back of the house. Todd turned the corner ahead of them, glancing back to make sure they were keeping up and pointing, even as he ran, at his brother.

I was out of the closet.

SEVEN

Men and heavy equipment orbited the house. I sat by myself on the bumper of a truck, draped in a blanket someone had given me. From the moment I first saw them rounding the garage, the fire crew hadn't paid me much attention. I was not of consequence. There was a fire. They had come to put it out.

A few years earlier, the family had gone to the Nevada State Fair, where they had a freefall ride. Todd being too scared, I was all the more adamant about wanting to go on it and I smiled as they locked me inside the cage. Soon I was alone, rocking gently at the top of the tower. I took in the crowded carnival scene below, all the colors and tunes. A pneumatic hiss and I disengaged, giving myself over to the mechanism, the situation, the familiar fate of things that go up. The cage smelled like cotton candy and puke.

Tonight, smoke was the only smell, but again I had given myself over.

Two hoses was all it took to drive the flames back to the closet from whence they came. The blaze was smothered as suddenly as it had come to life. Firemen stopped jogging and stood around.

Two of them came out into the yard near where I was sitting. They chatted with their backs to me. When they took off their helmets steam rose from their sweaty heads, and I overheard them saying something about the Giants. The captain walked alone through the back door with a clipboard and a walkie-talkie. He came back out a few minutes later, lit a cigarette, and held conference with a guy in a beige cargo vest. He shook Dad's hand, then climbed in his official red pickup and drove away.

Mom sat in one of the patio chairs, hugging Todd while absently stroking his hair. Dad carried the garden hose back across the yard and took the time to recoil it. I stood up from the bumper to help.

Oh no, he said. What you're doing is fine. Sit back down. Sit and think.

The man in the beige cargo vest walked up beside me. Under his vest he wore a dress shirt and a tie. He had a tidy gray beard, bright red lips, and reading glasses on a chain around his neck. He knew my name. He wiped soot off his hand onto his pants and held it out. I produced my own hand from inside the blanket and let him shake it. Hal McCormac, he said. He flipped open his wallet to reveal an ID and a badge. I glanced at it and read a couple of the words printed on it. One of the words caught my attention.

I've got a few questions, he said. Part of the procedure.

I didn't respond.

I'm sorry about your house, he said.

I checked out a couple library books the other day, I said. I just remembered. They were in my room.

Dad eyed us from the circuit box by the patio. He let go of the metal door and it swung shut with a clang. Inspector McCormac called over a fireman and told him to fetch some hot chocolate from a big thermos in his truck.

Want whipped cream? he asked me.

I don't want any hot chocolate, I said.

The fireman returned with a tray full of steaming Styrofoam cups. Mom and Todd took theirs in both hands, shivering. Dad nodded thank you but set his down on the table.

Arson, I said in a low voice. That's when someone starts a fire on purpose.

Mr. McCormac took a slurp of his chocolate and his beard scrunched up around his mouth as he savored it.

I took a look in that room of yours, he said, so I've got a decent idea what we're dealing with here. But I want to hear what you saw, what you noticed. I understand you were asleep when the fire started?

I get migraines.

You and my wife.

The fire was an accident.

How did it start?

Plus, it's not arson to burn down your own house, I said. Not always.

No?

No.

He studied me. I watched the zippers on his vest pendulate in unison whenever he moved. He jotted on his pad.

How about you tell me what you were keeping in your closet, he said.

By this point, many of our neighbors had gathered in the backyard. Some of them had been around the first time the house burned. The mood tonight was a little different than last time— more like a pyre than a bonfire. Kelly and his mom leaned against the kitchen window while she chatted with Mrs. Enid from next door. Kelly held his black standard poodle, Harold, on a leash. I looked at Kelly once and I could tell he'd been waiting to catch my eye, but I kept my head moving as if I hadn't seen him. A red light swept across the house, the grass, the pond, the trees. My headache had faded. I almost missed it. Inspector McCormac was still waiting.

Sodium, I said. He nodded, but I could see his nonchalance was an act. I wasn't twelve anymore. I felt the weight of my disclosure, the leverage I wielded.

Amazing stuff, he said.

I didn't say anything. I was a freak. A freak.

You've decided to be honest, he said. And that's good. It's going to make both of our nights a little shorter. I'm just trying to find out what happened, file my report, go home.

I'd wish I could go home, I said.

I understand, he said.

Nice as Inspector McCormac was, he didn't understand. But I was beginning to. Something inside me had come loose. I felt older, maybe. Detached from my first thirteen years. Right there in my backyard, sharing a cold metal bumper with an arson inspector, looking out over the remnants of a chaos I'd set in motion, I was suddenly just far away enough from the front of my life to see for the first time what it was.

Every once in a while, Dad unknowingly rented a movie that showed a little sex. Mom would grab the remote and fast-forward as soon as the kissing started. Lovemaking accelerated to epilepsy. The room would go quiet except for the sound of revving VCR heads. When the scene ended, Mom would push play and the story would resume, but how could we respect the characters anymore, having witnessed their naked spasm sandwich? And now, when I fast-forwarded my life, the countless explosions—so big and bright at the time—amounted to nothing more than a string of flickers. A lit fuse, burning its way toward what?

I told Inspector McCormac what I knew. He listened. During what seemed to me the least consequential parts of the story, he jotted. Meanwhile a pair of firemen leaned a ladder against the house and climbed up onto the shingles. I had to talk over the chainsaw while they cut a hole out of the roof like the lid of a jack-o-lantern. They reached into the hole to pull out soggy wads of scorched insulation.

I don't know what else there is, I said. That's what happened.

No, no, he said. That's fine. He flipped backward through his notepad, nodding to himself. He looked at me. Maybe he thought I was going to tell him something else.

Across the yard, Kelly remained beside his mother. She was chatting with a group, but Kelly stared out into the darkness beyond the pond. Harold the poodle waddled around, testing the radius of his leash, yanking Kelly's arm every which way. Kelly looked vulnerable, but perhaps only to me. I suppose the folks walking around Hiroshima only appeared vulnerable to the 12 guys looking down from the Enola Gay.

I had a migraine, I said.

I know, said Inspector McCormac. He patted my leg, got up, and went over to talk with Dad.

One of the fire engines left. A few guys from the original crew remained. They doused hot spots and rounded up equipment. I forced myself to relocate to the patio and take a seat next to Todd. Mom talked with a fireman while he held his helmet politely in his hands. He had a goatee and blue eyes. She wanted to know when she could start cleaning up.

We hit it pretty hard with the hoses, he said, which is good. Your house didn't burn down. But the place is flooded. People are always surprised when they go back because of the water. You can open the windows and try and dry it out, but you're gonna end up hiring a professional outfit. Insurance covers it.

Stan's in insurance, Mom said. My husband.

The water's the least of your worries, ma'am. It's the smell that's gonna haunt you. Smoke gets into everything. Your clothes, drapes, sheets, beds. It goes up the drains in your sinks and into the walls. It soaks into the pores in the wood.

We got my puzzles out, Mom said.

We noticed that, said the fireman. Hell of a trick.

Dad and the inspector were wrapping up. Dad offered his hand and the inspector moved his notepad under his other arm so he could shake it. Then he gathered up his things. I gave him a little wave, and he tipped the brim of an imaginary hat to me on his way out. Dad came over and put his arm around Mom.

We're just about done here, Mr. Brooks, the fireman said. I assume you've made arrangements.

Haven't you called the agency? Mom asked.

Not yet, Dad said. When no one spoke, he added that they wouldn't even be able to move on our claim until the morning at the earliest.

It is morning, Todd said. And we looked for ourselves at the purplish light creeping across the sky, the sharper outlines of the trees. Kelly and his mother were the only neighbors still there. She had been listening to our conversation and leaned in with a tentative smile.

I have a guestroom and plenty of couches, she said. I didn't want to leave until I knew ya'll had somewhere you could go.

Wow, the firemen muttered. Good neighbor.

Good neighborhood, Dad said proudly.

You folks can count your blessings, he said.

Yes, Mom said.

That's right, Dad said. His body drooped, his eyes hung wearily. That's right.

Todd tugged on my arm. He whispered something about his Halloween costume. I couldn't quite hear what he said. He wore his blanket like a hood, peering up at me from deep inside.

Are you in trouble, Oby? he whispered.

I nodded.

Tons?

You don't need to worry, I said. I could see his mind working to fathom the enormity of my mistake. I turned back to Mom and Dad's conversation. They were arguing about whether or not to call a hotel. When I looked down again Todd was crying.

I was almost at that point myself. Had I not seen the tears on my brother's face, I might have indulged in a few of my own. But it pissed me off seeing him that way. It seemed unnecessary, avoidable. And standing there helpless at the epicenter of it all, I punched a patio chair cushion.

———————————

At Mom's insistence, Dad, for the first time all night, sat down. She slipped in behind him on the lounge chair to rub his shoulders, but he didn't pay her much attention. He was still giving orders.

Todd, he said. Come on, pal. I know you're tired. You go with Mrs. Atkinson.

Todd still had the blanket over his head. Dad couldn't see he was crying. Mrs. Atkinson took Todd by the hand and, with a parting pat on Mom's shoulder, led him off, Kelly in tow.

Kelly turned back to look at me.

Aren't you coming? he asked.

I'd successfully eluded Kelly all night, leaving him blissfully unaware. I never told him I'd taken the blame for the way he'd put away the sodium. I never would. He had no idea what he'd set off. He was fragile and naïve and I liked it better that way. I dared not elevate him to the status of co-conspirator, knowing full well he'd savor such an alliance.

He'll be along shortly, Kelly, Dad said.

And the three of them disappeared around the corner of the house.

Sit down, Oby, Dad said when they were gone.

I'm okay, I said. I'll stand.

Sit, Mom said.

The metal footings of the patio chair scraped across the concrete as I pulled it out. As soon as I was sitting down Dad stood up
again. He began pacing. Mom kept her eye on him and I could see
she was comforted by his tight grip of the situation and the calm-
ness with which he now readied himself.

It's late, he began, and I'm exhausted. So is your mother. What
Mr. McCormac told us—it's disturbing. It's disturbing to hear that
your oldest son, the one who's supposed to be setting an example
for his brother, is going to such great lengths to hide something.
This demented little fascination of yours. It's not how your mother
and I raised you. Not at all.

He rubbed his hand on his whiskers and turned to look at the
yard. I could tell he was raging inside by the peaceful composure of
his face. Mom glanced at me for a second, her eyes helpless. She'd
become a witness to whatever happened here. Dad was in charge. I
couldn't look back at her. I had to look away.

Do you think it's strange at all? she asked. The way you are?

I don't think so, I said.

Do your friends keep bombs in their rooms?

Probably not, I said.

Where did you get it from? How are you like this?

This isn't why we're here, Dad said, shaking his head. This isn't
why we're here.

Mom pulled a blanket tight around her chest and looked away.

I haven't called in our claim yet, Dad said. I work with these
people for Christ's sake, I know how they operate.

The inspector said…

I know what the inspector said, Anne. But just because it
doesn't say arson in his report doesn't necessarily—

He stopped and collected himself, then continued.

Do you know what's going to happen when I call this in? They'll send out an adjuster. I'm guessing Kurt Wellans—who's a nice enough guy but he's good at what he does, and what he does is make certain that the company doesn't pay out unless it's supposed to. Do you know what a negligence exclusion is? Oby, I'll bet you can guess. You're Academically Gifted. So, what do you think an insurance company might think when they learn that you were hiding a highly reactive chemical in the house? Especially knowing full well what it could do because you'd seen a demonstration that day in school. Before you stole it.

Today, I thought. Since lunch. The whole world had burned since lunch.

Who knows, Dad said. They might even suspect fraud. I have burned the house down for money before!

I didn't speak.

Dad pointed at me. Tomorrow, he said, you and I are going to have a talk with this Mr. Weisgard. I have a few questions for him.

And I think a letter of apology is in order, Mom added.

To who? I asked.

Whom, Mom said. And Mr. Weisgard for starters.

It's a holiday, Dad, I said. Teachers aren't at school.

But I don't think he even heard me.

You might be interested to know, he said, that our insurance policy is void if a fire starts as a result of some kind of illegal action.

He stared at me. I sat hoping he didn't expect a reply, because I didn't have one.

The very most I could muster was half a shrug.

I'm going to bed, Dad said. He helped Mom out of her chair and put his arm around her waist and led her along the concrete path around the garage.

The horizon was stained pink. The sun was going to rise any

minute. I was the only one left. I rubbed my eyes. My fingers reeked of smoke. I heard something hissing, sensed a groundswell. Sprinkler heads began popping up all over the lawn.

EIGHT

Stretched from fist to fist across my shoulders, the donated blanket was thin and damp, the membranous wing of a newborn pterodactyl. There was a hint of smoke on my skin, in my clothes. My eyes were opening slowly. I would be wide awake in seconds but I let the blurriness linger for a few perfect moments before dread seeped back in.

I could hear birds and their stupid singsong, their rhetorical questions.

I *know*, I nearly told them.

The small couch where I'd made my nest was facing an oak television cabinet. On either side of the cabinet were bookshelves. There was no coffee table, just a rug on the floor. A pair of port windows near the ceiling let in sunlight, muted and orange. I tried to fall back asleep but it was no use. A few minutes later I sat up, tugged on my shoes and trudged into the kitchen to see what could be salvaged of the rest of my life.

Mrs. Atkinson was paying bills at the kitchen table, reading glasses perched at the tip of her nose.

Oby! she said. You startled me! She lowered her chin and looked me over. You must be starving, she said, and she poured me a bowl of Chex.

They tasted like soggy Triscuits. My taste buds were numb. Congestion dribbled down the back of my throat. I ate what I could, then took the bowl to the sink and let the omnivorous disposal eat the rest.

Oby, Mrs. Atkinson said.

Mm.

That's enough.

Mm?

That's enough!

The grinder was whirring, bone dry and unobstructed. I turned it off and it eventually spun to a stop. Mrs. Atkinson was staring at me so I looked away and studied my reflection in the oven door. The night before, when everyone had left and the sprinklers came on, I'd rushed into the house in search of something to put on over my boxers and T-shirt. I'd ended up in my parent's room. Their closet was smoky, but the clothes in their dresser hadn't smelled too bad. I'd grabbed an old pair of running shoes on the floor. Found a sweatshirt and some sweatpants. And, as it turned out, my makeshift ensemble was The Outfit. While unflatteringly tight on Dad, the cuffs billowed at my ankles and wrists.

Mrs. Atkinson took off her glasses and set her pen down.

Your mother left a few hours ago, she said. She wanted to get a head start on the cleaning. Your brother is still asleep.

Where's my Dad?

She smiled, put her glasses back on, and returned to her bills. I asked her again but she wouldn't look up. I turned around. Dad was standing behind me. He had a mug in his hand. I moved out of his way. He went straight to the coffee maker on the counter and poured himself a refill. A single drip of coffee escaped from the filter and sizzled on the hot plate.

Was the couch long enough for you, Oby? Mrs. Atkinson asked. Was it comfortable? I forget how much you boys have grown.

Dad answered for me. It was fine, he said. Just fine.

Good, she said. I'm glad.

He leaned against the counter and took a tentative sip of coffee, followed by a longer gulp.

Nice sweats, he said.

I kept quiet.

You ready to pay a visit to Mr. Weisgard? he said.

I don't know where he is, I answered.

I do, he said, nodding to a splayed-open phone book on the counter. He sipped his coffee.

I haven't written my apology letter.

Yeah, well, you can say you're sorry to his face, like a man.

Mom said...

I know what she said.

Do we really need to *go over there*? *Today*?

Yep, Dad said. I'm gonna find out about this sodium stuff he's got so I can argue with the insurance company without sounding like an idiot. And you need to say sorry so maybe this all stops there—he has every right to report you on Monday. Get the school district involved.

Before you go, Mrs. Atkinson said, maybe Oby ought to take a shower? Kelly would be happy to loan him some clothes.

Where is Kelly? I asked.

He waited around for you this morning, but you slept so long. The drama club is making a movie this afternoon at Gina Webster's house.

Oh, I said, realizing that by now the entire school probably knew.

Mr. Weisgard lived in a neighborhood we used to drive through on our way to T-ball games when I was a kid, back when the ball kept still, all juicy and ready to pound off the tee. On our drive over in the Wagoneer, Dad handed me the directions. He'd written them on a paper bag. So I became navigator. It gave us something to say to each other.

Right on Hunter Lane.

Hunter *Lake*. We're already on it.

Sorry. Left on California.

I know. Then what?

Left on... I couldn't read his handwriting. The turn signal clicked and clicked. It seemed to get faster.

Dad turned left. Left on what, Oby? I'm on California now.

I can't quite read what you wrote.

Just give it here.

Wait. I'll figure it out.

We're gonna miss our turn.

Whatever, I said, holding out the bag. He snatched it out of my hands.

WHUMP-WHUMP! Dad slammed the brakes.

Damn it, Oby!

What was that? I asked.

He adjusted the rear view mirror. Jesus! he said. It's a goddamn cat!

I spun in my seat and looked out the gigantic rear window. There in the road was a lump of black fur with a leg protruding at an aberrant angle and twitching. The lump squirmed then went still.

Dad pulled over. He got out and walked back to the cat. I didn't know what to do. He left his door ajar and it bing-bonged, bing-bonged, so I reached across and tugged it shut. Suddenly everything was quiet. A silent movie played on the big back window.

Dad was a mime. The mime toed the lump. Then the mime looked up and down the block. There was a schoolyard next to the road. The mime picked up the lump by what looked to be a tail, or maybe an intestine. There was a stain on the asphalt. The mime carried the cat at arm's length through a gate in the fence to a trash barrel on the playground and dropped it in. The mime rubbed his hands on his jeans and came back to the car. When the mime put his hand on the door the silent movie ended and brisk air rushed into the car. Dad turned on the heater.

Thing didn't have any tags, he said. Not even a collar.

So, what should we do? I asked.

He cupped his hands and smelled them.

What do you mean, *what should we do*, Oby? I just did it.

What if it's not dead?

It's dead.

How do you know?

How do I know. Let's see: how do I know. Well, the thing's head was half off, but you can go make sure if you like, doctor.

It's okay.

He looked at me. You're on quite a roll, he said. He picked up the directions. *Ferris*, he said. Left on *Ferris*. It's perfectly legible.

He dropped the crinkled bag in my lap and we drove away. I considered tugging the handle and ejecting myself from the Wagoneer, wondering if I could Rambo roll at 40 mph, but Mr. Weisgard's house was only a block from the intersection. We'd parked before I had time to garner the resolve.

It was a small house, similar to all the others on the block but with greener grass. We went to the door.

Whoever cuts this lawn uses an edger, Dad said.

Mm, I said. I had on Kelly's rayon shirt, and every time I moved it released a faint waft of cologne.

He rang the doorbell. We heard feet stampeding across hardwood floors. The door swung open. A pair of boys, both younger than I, stood before us. A little girl peeked her head out between them. She wore a skeleton mask. All three of them had on pajamas.

Who is it? someone yelled from inside the house.

The oldest boy asked us who we were. Dad introduced himself, then he introduced me. The boy relayed our names at nearly the top of his lungs. The little girl peeled back the skeleton mask so I could see her face and she smiled at me. I couldn't bring myself to smile back. She stuck out her tongue.

Okay, came a voice from deep inside the house. A voice I recognized.

The boys stood down. They ushered us into the threshold and offered to take our coats. The rooms in the house were quaint and clean except for a study, where a bulky wood desk was littered with magazines, journals, spiral notebooks, and mechanical odds and ends. The boys led us down a hallway covered with framed photos. One of them showed Mr. Weisgard in full mountain man garb, flanked by his sons, one in a beige Boy Scout uniform, the other in a blue Cub Scout shirt. The boys had patches and sashes and scarves and epaulets galore. I knew as soon as I saw the picture that Dad would point it out. He was always looking for ways to refute my contention that Todd and I were the only boys still in Scouts.

Do you guys have a cat? Dad asked the oldest boy.

Are you allergic or something? he replied. My mom is. She has special medicine.

What color is the cat?

Carbon? He's black. He's not really our cat, though. He sort of roams.

We came into the kitchen and adjoining dining room. Mr. Weisgard stood behind a dinner table covered in newspaper. He wore a chef's apron.

Mr. Oby, he said. And Mr. Brooks.

In his left hand, a knife, and in his right a big metal spoon. A pair of jack-o-lanterns stared at their own freshly spilled guts. One smiled, the other grimaced.

I'd shake your hands, but…

No, no, Dad said.

The boys like cutting out the faces, Mr. Weisgard said. Seems like I always end up doing the scooping.

Ain't that the truth, Dad said.

Mr. Weisgard picked up another pumpkin. His wrist twisted and jerked, scraping the hollow cavity. He flung the slop into a pile, then cleared away newspaper and gestured to a pair of chairs.

We won't be long, Dad said.

Coffee? Mr. Weisgard asked.

I probably shouldn't, Dad said. I drank my share this morning. Didn't sleep a whole lot last night, so I've been running on caffeine.

Godsend of a molecule, Mr. Weisgard said.

Dad folded his hands in his lap and a grave look crept across his face. He looked for a moment at the two boys and the little girl hovering at the end of the table. He rubbed his knees. The only sound was Mr. Weisgard's incessant scraping. After a while he looked up and saw us staring at him. He set down his spoon.

Boys, he said, how about you take Joyce-Ann and go help Mom?

———————

The pumpkins kept an eye on us while Mr. Weisgard went to wash his hands. Dad said not a word to me. All along, I'd been expecting him to prep me for our encounter, to tell me to look Mr. Weisgard in the eye and how to word my apology—put the ball on the tee—but nope.

Mr. Weisgard came back without his apron. I'd seen other in-carnations of Mr. Weisgard: mountain man, mad scientist, pumpkin carver, and now this, with his flannel sleeves rolled up and a mug of steaming coffee in his hands. He plunked down the mug and crossed his legs. Dad wasn't going to speak first. I realized who would. I cleared my throat.

I hope this isn't about Oby stealing sodium chloride, Mr. Weisgard said. He looked at us both in turn and laughed invitingly, expecting us to join in.

Dad pointed at him. You knew that? he said.

Of course, Mr. Weisgard said. He kept on laughing.

I joined in, just a little. Dad didn't.

My son thinks this is funny, he said. I guess I'm the only one who finds it completely disturbing!

Mr. Brooks, I would ask you to lower your voice in my house…

Who the hell lets a 13-year-old boy steal sodium?

Chloride, Mr. Weisgard added. Please tell me you've interrupted my holiday over more than a pinch of salt?

How can you be so casual?

Is this a joke?

Things escalated from there. Mr. Weisgard called Dad a lunatic. Dad said Mr. Weisgard was no better than a drug dealer. I said nothing. I could have fessed up immediately and prevented the whole mix-up, but each passing insult only compounded the consequence of interrupting. Throughout it all—even when Mr. Weisgard hinted at the shortcomings of Dad's education—Dad never mentioned that our house had burned, maybe because that particular detail was to be the foundation upon which I built my forthcoming apology. He did, however, call Mr. Weisgard unfit to teach kids, or raise them.

To defuse the situation, I told Mr. Weisgard the awful truth.

I think we ran over your cat, I said. My dad left it in a barrel down the street.

Mr. Weisgard's expression was caught in transition between indignation and befuddlement.

Dad nodded solemnly. A big black fella, he said. Sort of mangy?

Mr. Weisgard stood up from the table and left the room without another word. Dad looked at me. I don't think he knew what to say. I'd beaten him to the punch. I'd owned up before Mr. Own Up himself.

Mr. Weisgard walked back into the dining room. Draped over his arm was a cat. Like our victim this cat was black. Unlike our victim, it was three-dimensional.

Carbon's right here, Mr. Weisgard said, and he smiled as if he felt sorry for us. I don't know what kind of scam this is, but I want you both out of my house.

Fine, Dad said. He got up from the table. Let's go, Oby.

I stayed put. We're not talking about salt, I said.

Mr. Weisgard kept stroking Carbon. Dad pushed in his chair, but didn't let go of it.

I stole some of the pure sodium, I said. I took it out of the classroom while you were playing soccer. I brought it home on the bus, and I left it in my closet and it started a fire. A pretty big one. Actually, part of my house burned down.

It was the Cliff's Notes version, hitting the main points, glossing over the morals. Strangely, it felt like boasting. I looked at Dad.

I came here to say I'm sorry.

Not to me, Dad said. To him.

Sorry, I said. I turned to look Mr. Weisgard right in the eye. I could only return his gaze for a few seconds, so I settled on looking him in the mustache. I'm sorry, I said.

The nodding of Mr. Weisgard's head looked animatronic, disengaged. Your house *burned*, he mumbled.

Okay, Dad said. Thank you, Oby. Now go sit in the car.

He tossed me the keys.

By myself? I said.

You've said what you came here to say.

Mr. Weisgard took a sip of his coffee and paused to stare out the window into his backyard. I didn't catch his eye as I left the room. But I didn't try.

Had I known just how long I was going to be in the car, I would have come up with some way to pass the time. As it was, I must have stared out the window for half an hour, insulated from all sounds, feeling no breeze. It was a Jeep aquarium. Mothers with strollers and kids on bikes and people in cars—everyone looked in at me. Once, I smiled at a jogger to quell his suspicion, to show him that a parked car in a quiet neighborhood is an ordinary place to spend an afternoon alone. He kept running.

Eventually, the thought crossed my mind to get out of the car, stroll around, but I couldn't risk being A.W.O.L. when Dad came back. I rummaged through the glove box and found three virtually identical Nevada highway maps. I unfolded one across the dashboard and imagined the liberation I would feel in three years when I could put key to ignition and pick any road—the one to Tonopah, or Vegas, or out of Nevada all together—and go. Turn the wheel and push the pedal and follow a road. I always watched closely when Mom or Dad drove and thought I knew what to do.

I found a ballpoint pen and, in the vast and desolate expanse of my home state, practiced my signature. Just north of Pioche I experimented with spherical and ovular O's and tried various loops for the tails of my Y's, a few times letting it swoop all the way around my name.

I thought about the dead cat. I wondered if there really was good and bad luck, or if what happened *before* was always the explanation for what came *after*. Was there a reason the cat died under the Wagoneer? A purpose? If so, I didn't see it. Seemed like the cat just decided to cross the road at the same time we decided to drive down it—a mundane choice, like the purchase of an M-80 or the pilfering of salt, but still a *choice*.

My thoughts then turned to the fire. But I realized that's what Dad intended for me to do in the car, so I tried to fall asleep and not think about anything. But I was too cold to get comfortable. The windows fogged up. I stared in turn at a basketball net partially unhooked from its rim, a resilient weed rooted in a sidewalk crack, an archipelago of driveway stains. The neighborhood was a still life. If you gave me a canvas and some brown, yellow, and green paint I could paint it today, from memory. Somewhere, not too far away, grommets clanged against a flagpole. The noise came and went. It would slip away, then I'd realize it had never stopped. I'd just stopped hearing it.

Finally, Dad came out onto the porch, followed by Mr. Weisgard, who leaned against the door, arms folded. They shook hands. I hastily refolded the map and stuffed it back into the glove box. Mr. Weisgard pointed with his hand at something distant. Dad nodded, laughing. I put on my seatbelt, unaware that it would be another five minutes of chatting before Dad finally shook Mr. Weisgard's hand *again* and returned to the Wagoneer.

You were in there for a long time, I said.

Yeah? Dad said. Mmm.

NINE

Mom insisted we eat some fruit with our pizza, so Mrs. Atkinson took a few bunches of purple grapes out of the fridge. We ate off of paper plates. There weren't enough chairs at the kitchen table for all eight of us, (Kelly's two older sisters were home), so Kelly and I leaned against the counter. Mom told us about her day cleaning the house. She'd just gotten back.

The smoke smell isn't *that* bad, she said. It's getting better.

Sweetie, you reek, Dad said. You probably got desensitized being in there so long.

She took a long sip of Diet Coke. Might explain my headache, she said.

I want you to know, Mrs. Atkinson said, that ya'll are welcome to stay here as long as you need.

Dad set down his slice like he was going to make an announcement. He put his napkin over his mouth. After a while he swallowed and said that after dinner he was going to call Kurt and file the claim to get things rolling.

Honey, Mom said. It's after 5:00.

I'm going to call him at home, Dad spoke with authority, his confidence having swelled somehow inside Mr. Weisgard's house. He had a new swagger, so I kept my mouth shut lest I take a tomahawk to the chest. I stuffed my plate in the trash under the sink and excused myself. Kelly asked where I was going. Everyone tuned in.

I'm going to walk over there, I said.

Have you written your apology letter yet? Mom asked.

I will, I muttered.

Good idea, Dad said. Go take a look. When you get back, we'll talk.

This upset Todd.

Aren't we trick-or-treating? he asked.

It's not even dark yet, Dad said.

Mom patted Todd on the arm.

I still need to wash your costume, sweetie. It's all smoky.

I was eager to be alone, to indulge in a few salty moments of self-pity. But Kelly tagged along. We walked down the side of the road. I had my hands in the pouch of one of the sweatshirts I'd borrowed from him and my head cinched inside the hood. It smelled faintly of cologne. I couldn't see Kelly beside me, just the stone he kept kicking.

Stop, I said.

What's your problem?

Stop kicking that rock.

He kicked it into the ditch.

Though I knew better, I half expected to find a blackened framework at the end of my driveway, wisps of smoke rising from rubble. But the house looked cozy and inviting. Mom had left some lights on. I hadn't ruined *everything*. I'd ruined 15 percent of everything.

You can't tell, I said. The front of the house looks the same.

Yeah, Kelly said. I saw this movie once where a guy gets a pistol shoved in his mouth, but even when his brains get blasted all over the wall behind him, his face looks fine. It's kind of like that.

We walked around the side of the house. Kelly nudged my elbow and pulled a small white tube out of his pocket. I had a feeling it wasn't a cigarette because it was crinkled and bulbous, like a piece of candy rolled up in paper.

Want to? he said.

What is it?

Weed.

No way. Let me see.

I held it in my open palm and stared at it from different angles, as if it were a captured grasshopper. I asked him where he'd gotten it.

A guy at school, he said. You wouldn't know him.

What's that supposed to mean?

Kelly pinched it up to his nose and took a sniff. Here, he said, light it.

What's it like?

Mellow.

My parents would pretty much kill me, I said.

They'll never know, he said. Just spray yourself with some of this. He held out a square green bottle of Polo cologne.

Let's get behind the house, I said.

On the back porch he lit the joint. He took two long drags, started coughing and handed it to me in his fingertips. I took it and tried a drag.

You didn't get any in your lungs, Kelly said.

So, I sucked harder, and I started coughing too.

Hell yeah, he said. One more, just like that.

Pretty soon I was above myself, looking down. Laughing. Wondering who else was looking down at me. We passed the joint back and forth. It dwindled in stops and starts into ash, an impetuous fuse.

You've got to tell me how it went, he said.

Yeah? I asked, lost.

The fire, he continued.

But I didn't want to talk about it. I wasn't sure what I'd say. I felt vulnerable. Kelly had found a way to gain a chemical advantage on me.

Something in my closet just started burning, I said.

The sodium, right? It was the sodium! Oby, what did you tell them?

Nothing.

You kicked me out, man. I tried covering it up in that plastic bag…

Kelly, shut the fuck up.

How did it start burning?

Maybe the moisture in the air. Does it even matter?

Is that what you told the inspector?

The inspector wasn't stupid. He already knew everything.

About me?

About you? Kelly, no one cares about *you*! I said it was my fault. It's always my fault. Don't worry your pretty little head. Just stop talking.

I'm sorry it happened, though. I feel bad for you.

You don't know shit.

We sat in silence. Sweet smoke lingered. Kelly flipped me off and we started to laugh, and then we started coughing, and then laughing a little more.

I'm starving, Kelly said. Any Vienna sausage in your house?

Are you serious?

Do you think you'll have to go off to some correctional school? Like Rhett Cohen?

Didn't that guy steal a car?

I think so, Kelly said. I guess that's different. You just blow shit up.

Fuck off.

Asshole.

He got up and walked around the side of the house. Five minutes later, he hadn't come back. I felt very alone. I couldn't see anyone watching me, but I knew *someone* was. I was on some hidden security camera, or the neighbors saw me through slats in the fence. Maybe someone in a hot air balloon. I got up and walked into the yard. I was acutely aware of the expression on my face and the way I swung my arms. I was on stage. It was brutal paranoia. I needed, for this particular scene, to exude remorse. I hung my head.

It wasn't entirely for show. Truly, I wanted to travel back in time to when I stole the sodium. No—further back, to the family trip to San Francisco and the Chinatown alleyway I found while I was supposed to be at the arcade, the collapsible street booth bursting with all things pyrotechnic, where I squandered three months of allowance. Or all the way back to the shed, where I perfected my recipe for napalm.

Name one guy on planet Earth. At that moment, I would have swapped places with him. In the paper I'd seen a picture of some Chinese guy standing in the street, about to be run over by a column of advancing tanks. *Him.*

I crept up to my window. Charred slabs of broken siding snapped under my feet. I looked in and saw ashes floating in puddles. My room had been a shelter from the universe. There, a Walkman piped Top 40 directly to my eardrums. There, I closed my eyes and whispered along. My clothes. Old movie tickets, my tennis racket, posters. How the hell could I show people what I was about if I didn't have stuff? Without Nikes, I felt naked.

I sat on the lawn, posing in such a way that if Dad had come upon me he would have believed I was contemplating my mistake. Water from the thawing grass crept through Kelly's cords and chilled my skin. I jumped up. Academically Gifted! I took off Kelly's sweatshirt and tied it around my waist so that it concealed the wet spots.

The back door was locked. So was the front door, and the one on the side of the garage. I went back to my window and climbed in, careful not to slice my palms. Black water oozed from my carpet wherever I stepped. In the hallway there were axe holes and charred slabs of sheetrock. I'd walked from my room to the kitchen so many times before; now it felt like breaking and entering. A gust of wind pushed through the house, flipping pages of a *National Geographic* on the coffee table. I went in my parents' room, found some type of cologne on their dresser and spritzed it liberally all over myself. My sneezes echoed in the empty house. At the end of the hallway I took off my shoes. I dared not track soot across Mom's newly laid vacuum swaths.

The house didn't feel like mine. The portrait hanging in the hall seemed to be of some other family, maybe the one that came with the frame. There was a mother and a father, their embrace encompassing two sons kneeling on thick blue carpet. Certainly, I had not chosen this family. I had been born into it. My genes were hand-me-downs. What an arbitrary and unjust arrangement! Couldn't I have ended up being *any* boy in *any* family picture in the world? Had Kelly popped out of Mom almost 13 years ago, would he be standing in a half-charred house instead? Would he savor the aroma of kerosene?

I mixed a pitcher of Crystal Light and drank two glasses in the dark. After a while I heard voices in the front yard. The doorbell rang. I feared it was Todd, come to fetch me. Or maybe Kelly, hungry for sausage and abuse. I looked through the window. A threesome in masks and capes crowded the porch. I went to the door.

Pillowcases gaped like gullets.

Trick or treat!

A man waved to me from a minivan idling in the driveway. He wished me a happy Halloween. I looked at the kids. They stared back. One of them reiterated my options: Trick, or treat.

Hold on, I said.

I dashed into the house, skating to a halt across the kitchen linoleum. I lifted the lid of the cookie box. Nothing. No sweets in the candy basket. We didn't even have granola bars or fruit roll ups. I found only wheat bread and spices in the pantry. Seconds slipped away. I had to find treats. At that moment I needed nothing more. Three normal kids on my doorstep had come expecting a normal thing from a normal house. They had no idea what breed of drugged-out freakizoid had answered the door, or that the house's brains were blown out. I hadn't done a normal thing in at least 24 hours. I had to do a normal thing.

I found what I was looking for and scrambled back, reining in my pace before reaching the foyer. I forced myself to breathe normally. But the kids were already retreating. One of them was halfway back to the minivan. The father noticed me and pointed. They all came scrambling back to the door and stood at attention while I played papa bird, stuffing their quivering beaks with cans of Vienna sausage. The tallest of the three reached into his pillowcase. He pulled his can back out to look it over, quizzically.

The father waved again. What do we say? he hollered.

I walked back to the Atkinson's. The fuzziness of the joint was wearing off. Chaperoned pods of trick-or-treaters were fleecing the neighborhood, shortcutting lawns. I got to the Atkinson's house at the same time as Batman, a fairy, and Optimus Prime. The fairy and I reached for the doorbell simultaneously and I touched her glove.

What are you? Optimus gawked at me.

The female voice came as a surprise. Across her breast was a windshield with tiny wipers. Exhaust pipes protruded from her shoulders.

Oh, I said. I'm nothing.

Really? She pointed her hand-cannon at the sweatshirt around my waist. I thought that was a skirt, she said. Are you getting candy?

No, I'm coming home.

Why'd you ring the doorbell? Can't you just go in?

It's not my house.

Silence. I smiled. Optimus Prime was clearly annoyed and turned to stare at the door.

I guess I do have a costume, I muttered, half to myself. I'm Kelly.

Kapowski?

I was going to be A.C. Slater, Batman said, but my mom says I look more like Zack. I hate Zack.

No, no, I said. Different Kelly. A boy Kelly. He lives here. These are his clothes. I wouldn't wear this stuff. Normally.

Optimus Prime leaned an ear against the door. Shh, she said. Someone's coming.

The door opened. Mrs. Atkinson stood before us with a bowl of Laffy Taffy on her hip. I ducked past her and went straight into the family room. Everyone was watching TV. A balding interrogator yelled questions at a man handcuffed to a chair. The man in the chair wouldn't so much as blink, infuriating the interrogator. Mom and Dad snuggled together on the couch. Todd and Kelly were sprawled on the carpet. Kelly discretely flipped me off.

Dad took his arm off Mom's shoulder and patted her leg as he stood up from the couch. Kelly slithered across the carpet and up to Dad's empty spot on the couch beside Mom.

Ready to talk? Dad asked.

I walked ahead of Dad down the hallway. I didn't want to go into Kelly's room, or Mrs. Atkinson's bedroom, or the bathroom. The laundry room seemed somewhat private, so I went in there and Dad followed. Todd's costume, a Will Clark uniform, made random clicks as it flopped around in the dryer.

I called Kurt, Dad said. He'll be over in the morning to assess the damage. From what it sounds like, your closet probably won't be an issue. Are you wearing Mom's perfume?

No.

He looked at me sideways. Well, he said, Mr. Weisgard tells me that sodium gets sent through the mail—which strikes me as idiotic. But having it around isn't *illegal* as I understand it, just dangerous in the wrong hands, like a rope, or gasoline.

Or a glass of water, I thought. I asked him how long I was going to be grounded.

That's why we're here, right? Dad said. You and me. In the Atkinson's laundry room.

He rested a hip against the washing machine. Losing your room and all your things—that's one punishment, he said. But you know me: I'm looking for something we can take away from this. If I ground you, Mom and I will end up watching you sulk around the house for months.

Months?

I think all your sulking led us to this. Have you considered that? Or is blowing stuff up some kind of weird outlet for you? Hell, all boys play with fire. I did. But I never made any damn *napalm*.

He looked me over for a moment.

Stay here, he said, and left. I listened to the dryer. By the time he got back I had deciphered something of a rhythm in its erratic rumble-tumble. He had a thin stack of books in his hand.

I don't think I ever told you about the time your grandpa caught me spitting, he said. I was in Little League. I'd seen players on TV with their tobacco, spitting all over the dugout. I guess that's where I picked it up—who knows. But when Grandpa saw me, well, he was the coach and he yanked the helmet off my head and took me out of the batting order.

Spitting is for camels and assholes, he told me.

Dad's spot-on impression of grandpa seemed to catch us both off guard, and we shared an unexpected laugh. Which, frankly, felt unprofessional. Where was my lashing?

Grandpa sent me back to the dugout, Dad continued, with an empty bottle of booze from the trash. Brought it over and dropped it in my lap.

Fill that with spit and you can play.

Dad laughed at himself again. I held back, for fear this scene was quickly becoming an outtake—we'd have to shoot it again: it wasn't convincing. Damn it, Dad. Flog me! My tears will boil as dignity sustains me. I will clench my teeth at each crack of the whip. Watch me take my thrashing like a man. Please. Give me something to take my mind off the guilt that keeps creeping in, whenever I stop to think. A beating.

Disgusting, Dad continued. That bottle was all sticky and every time I put my lips near it I'd smell the booze. I spit until my mouth was dry. Grandpa made me take it home and finish. Took a couple days. *You're gonna spit as well as a camel or you're never gonna spit again—one or the other.* The bottle was always a little warm and it smelled like whatever I'd been eating, and even now when I spit out my toothpaste I remember it.

Jeez, I said.

This *hobby* of yours, it doesn't seem healthy, Oby. But Mr. Weisgard tells me there's actually *jobs*—good-paying ones—in explosives. Not just in the army. Although maybe the army would do you some good, you keep this up.

What are those? I asked, nodding at the books in his hand.

These are from Mr. Weisgard's personal library, Dad said.

He handed them to me and I looked them over. Four in all. Chemistry merit badge handbook. Fire Safety merit badge handbook.

Atomic energy? I said.

Surprised me too, Dad said. Cooking was Mr. Weisgard's idea. None of these are required for Eagle, so you'll still have to work on those at troop meetings. These you finish on your own time.

I began leafing through the various requirements:

Name the most frequent causes of fire in the home and give examples of ways it can be prevented. Explain the role of human behavior in the arson problem in this country. Demonstrate the safe way to fuel a lawnmower. How does the safe storage of chemicals apply to your home, your school, your community, and the environment? Make a drawing showing how a chain reaction could be started…

So, this is my punishment?

If that's how you see it.

I listened to the laundry. Dad walked away.

TEN

When you blunder, you learn who your real friends are.

I learned I didn't have any. I returned to school on Monday, after the long Halloween weekend. The vice-principal pulled me aside on my way to homeroom. I scanned the hall to see who'd noticed. Her eyes were branding irons. I kept very still. She lay a hand on my shoulder with practiced sincerity. If there's anything we can do, she said, nodding.

There is, I thought. Let me rejoin the herd.

She continued nodding. She didn't stop nodding until I nodded back. Okay, she said, giving my arm a gentle squeeze.

Later that morning, I got pulled out of English to greet a special ed class in the hall. They'd collaborated on a gigantic poster/card scrawled with well-wishes and condolences. Someone had drawn a horse in ballpoint pen. Someone else had written simply, *Have Nice*. Below the horse was a brown figure drawn with crayon and wearing some kind of yellow hat. I swear it resembled Smokey Bear.

Then the lunch bell sounded, and I hardened myself for the encounter I'd been dreading more than any other. I arrived in the cafeteria to find the guys slouching around our usual table like a huddling football squad. Val was our quarterback. I rooted through my lunch bag and waited to see who'd fire first. Across the table, Richardson wrestled with a hamburger, ketchup hemorrhaging. I pecked at a blueberry muffin.

Kyle put a quarter on the table and set it spinning on its edge. He started counting. When he got to five, Val, sitting to Kyle's left, reached out and flicked the tottering coin. It spun with new life. We took turns. Each of us counted, then flicked, until, ironically, Kyle's mistimed finger sent his own quarter swerving lopsidedly to the floor under the drinking fountain. Val fetched it. Dutiful as ever, Kyle mashed his fist against the tabletop and awaited his due. Val zinged the quarter like a puck into Kyle's knuckle, splitting the skin.

We went back to eating. Val pushed a half-eaten basket of fries to the middle of the table. During the frenzied Hungry Hungry Hippos session that ensued, Richardson's hand somehow momentarily ended up in Val's mouth.

You bit me! Richardson said, examining his fingers. I'm bleeding!

Val took a look and shook his head. That's just ketchup, he said as a wad of potato fell out of his mouth and stuck to the table.

Tom pointed at the wad. I'll eat that for 10 bucks, he said.

Yeah? Val said, adding some mayonnaise and three packets of pepper, upping the stakes but not the cash prize. He told Richardson to go find some salt. Richardson got up. Val turned to me.

Heard you had a fire at your house this weekend, he said.

It felt as if they'd all been waiting for this question. A silence befell the table, a palpable ceasefire. All punching, chewing, and swearing stopped.

Richardson gave up on the salt and sat back down. Someone said you started it, he said. Is that true?

Yeah, Tom chimed in. Is that true?

Sort of, I said.

And I told them the story.

Holy shit, Richardson said when I was finished. So, are you in trouble?

Pretty much, I said. I opened my raisins and pried a few from the box-shaped clump they'd assumed. I didn't feel like saying anything else. Apparently, no one else did either.

Dude, Tom said, eying the wad. I'll still eat that shit.

No drinking anything, Richardson said.

And no plugging your nose, Val added.

I don't give a shit, Tom said.

Of course, it came as no surprise when a few years later Tom's parents bought him a pickup with oversized tires. The vanity plates spelled out some vowel-deficient summary of Tom's stance on fear, or total lack of fear, I can't remember. By then Tom and I weren't friends anymore. I wasn't friends with any of them. I never really was.

The next day, I sat through the entire lunch period without uttering a word. Kyle didn't say anything either, but he never did. And from that point on it became my little experiment, a solo stunt, to sit with them and say nothing. I pulled it off two days in a row. Then three. I felt like a chaperone. I even stopped listening to them and started watching people at other tables.

I'd always assumed we drew attention, that while we ganged up on each other and bloodied our knuckles, the rest of the lunchroom was watching, jealously entertained. But, nope. Aside from occasional glares of contempt from girls within our blast radius, no one gave a shit. Our cannibalism was self-contained. Piranha in a tank.

About a week into my experiment, I arrived at lunch to see the guys making their way to a different table. I started across the lunchroom to join them, realizing midway there that the table had only four open seats. Pac-man himself could not have navigated the right-angled lunch-table game board as fast as I did in my dash for the exit. I found myself in the hallway. Kids were still visiting their lockers, but the bell would ring any minute and the halls would be off limits during the lunch period. I ducked into an empty bathroom and shut myself in a stall.

Worried a teacher would catch me hiding there, I dropped my pants and tried to crap out an alibi. Soon, I was crying. A pair of janitors burst in. I hushed up while they used the urinals and joked with each other. After they were gone, I blew my nose into industrial toilet paper and cried harder, only quieter, and decided I might as well eat my lunch. I didn't get up until I heard the bell. My legs had fallen asleep.

Two weeks straight I ate lunch in that stall, my pants at my ankles. When next I showed my face in the lunchroom I felt like a new student. I sat down at a table with a bunch of rejects I'd never seen before. Turns out, there was an anonymous army of cast-outs who, like me, ate lunch at different tables every day. We didn't say much to anyone. At least, I didn't. I tried to keep at least one empty seat on either side of me. That way it looked like I was waiting on someone. A few times, I took the illusion so far as to turn away people who needed a seat.

Though I did my best to avoid him, Kelly snuck up behind me one day at the condiment counter.

Where you sitting? he asked.

Where *you* sitting? I countered.

He nodded to a nearby table. Two of Kelly's drama club pals were there already, arguing.

You like those guys? I said.

They're entertaining, he said. Sometimes I feel like their babysitter.

I laughed to myself as I pumped mustard into a paper cup. With a parting nod, I walked off—my gait suggesting purpose. I ate my corndog as I went, dunking it in mustard between bites, and in a single circumnavigation of the lunchroom the stick was clean.

I'd hit on a new way to avoid sitting alone: eat standing up.

I still had AG. A few of the others had dropped it. They didn't like being away from friends and dances and assemblies and all that. Of course, my sanctioned absence from these very things was one of the main reasons I'd never quit AG. My grades, which had already been pretty good, got even better. One week our AG mentor was a professor of economics and she talked about how causes are often confused with effects. It's true. A lot of people think smart kids end up geeks. But I think I speak for most of us when I say we're not geeks because we're smart; we're smart because we're geeks. We inherited neither sitcom wit nor soap-commercial skin; we lack the popularity-boosting types of coordination (hand-eye for boys, color for girls); we fixate on the smell of the webbing between our fingers. And eventually we're left alone, so we embrace education. I studied for the same reasons I jerked off: a lack of better prospects. Boredom.

Mom asked me why I stayed home every afternoon and weekend. Homework provided me with a bulletproof explanation. She praised my studiousness. She said I was diligent, and I was. I was a diligent little dork.

ELEVEN

I slept on a roll-away bed in Todd's room for a month. Without a place of my own in the house, I escaped on foot, taking almost daily walks. The world felt schizophrenic. Colors changed, temperatures wavered, and at night the wind howled in frightening tantrums, only to fall still at sunrise and leave the neighborhood looking like a scattered jigsaw puzzle.

I got around to writing an apology letter to Mr. Weisgard, using the same template as I used for thank-you notes: *Dear So and So, Thank you for the so and so. I really like it.* Only instead of thank you I said sorry and instead of liking it I regretted it. I found myself wishing there existed a punctuational opposite to the exclamation point.

I gave the letter to Mom and she said it could be longer.

The insurance company replaced all that was replaceable in my room, minus the deductible. That $300 was to come out of my hide—call it the Punitive Damage Merit Badge. They cut Mom a check and she took me to Mervyns on a shopping spree. We came home with a Wagoneer's worth of tube socks, stone-washed jeans, sweatshirts, sweatpants, tighty-whities, topsiders, tennis shoes, slippers, a parka—everything. I couldn't find T-shirts with logos I liked, so I bought a three-pack of plain gray, a pack of black, and one more of white.

You need a suit, Mom said.

For what?

Special occasions, weddings, church...

We don't go to church.

We used to. Maybe we should.

I don't want a suit.

We went to Macy's. As soon as we walked in, a salesman glided our way. His nametag said Jerry. He wore gold rings on just about every finger and a tape measure around his neck. Mom told Jerry I needed a suit.

Every man does, he said. Every man does.

He stood behind me, tracing tape along my limbs, whispering dimensions, then helped me into a grayish two-button number. The pleated pants hung past my heels and pooled on the carpet. A legion of clones moved at my whim in the tri-faceted dressing room mirror. We held out our arms in perfect unison.

Not bad, Mom said.

He's all shoulders, noted Jerry, chalking a few lines on the fabric.

It itches, I said.

You look nice, Mom said. She told Jerry to leave some room in the waist, then slipped away to scavenge the dress shirt displays.

We walked out of Macy's with the suit and matching ties, socks, shoes, and a reversible brown/black belt. Also, a blue blazer. The bill amounted to nearly $600, undoubtedly the most expensive shopping trip of my life. The stupid suit alone cost $330.

To pay down my $300 debt I worked in the yard for five dollars an hour. I drained the pond and shoveled out scum. I cut and stacked firewood. I replanted the burned-out hedgerow outside my room. I pulled weeds from under a big evergreen, then rolled out overlapping swaths of black plastic and covered it all with a thick layer of decorative bark. I hauled everything in the garage out into the driveway and swept the parking stalls, the broom kicking up dust and pollen. I sneezed in fits and rubbed my eyes until everything was blurry.

Dad had planted a border of crab apple trees along the western line of our property. The saplings needed frequent watering. I lugged the hose across a field of weeds dried yellow by the sun. Foxtails and goat-heads clung to my socks, pricked my legs. The hose didn't reach so I dragged another one from around the house. I screwed them together and opened the spigot. The hose got kinked. I pulled and whipped at it and it unkinked, then kinked again.

Fucking goddamn piece of shit, I growled.

The bitterness I felt was a heat-seeking missile launched into empty sky. It darted around for a target.

I threw down the hose at the base of the first tree in the row. Tiny bubbles of self-pity rose to the surface. I lay on my back in the dirt. The weeds bristled against my exposed legs and arms. I closed my eyes, but instead of black I saw pink—my eyelids translucent in the sun.

I readied myself for the moment Mom got home. She was going to be hugging grocery bags and saying something to Todd about what she would make him for his snack. She'd notice a boy toe-up in her yard, his face a big blister with a mouth, a defenseless kid who should never have been made to work under the noon sun. She cries out, *Oby!* And the groceries drop from her arms. Jars burst against the sidewalk. She rushes to my side and shoos the flies and plucks my flaccid body from the ground. She takes me inside and elevates my legs, drapes cool washcloths across my forehead. I am beyond reproach. Dad gets home from work and sees me sprawled out, my eyes recessed, my breath labored. Mom throws herself against him and pounds his chest as he tries to restrain her. *My boy!* she sobs. *What have we done? What have we done?* So Dad drops to his knees and weeps, the mere sight of me flooding him with biblical regret.

I awoke when the water overflowed the tree well and started to pool below me, soaking my clothes. Less than 20 minutes had gone by. It wasn't even that hot out. I stood up, looked around, and moved the hose to the next tree.

<hr>

Often, I fell asleep on top of my bed covers wearing my dirty work clothes and Mom would wake me up for dinner. I'd sit at the table and eat with the family, though I was beginning to feel like the maltreated stepchild, while my stepbrother, Todd—the *real* son— chatted away about himself and avoided his vegetables to the delight of our parents.

In the shower I'd noticed the emergence of soft black hair in my armpits. I yanked out every last one, leaving a rash where the roots had been.

By then I was mowing and trimming the lawn once a week. When the frost came and the grass stopped growing, I lowered the blade one setting and mowed again. Three weekends in a row I did that, trimming the dormant grass closer and closer to the ground. I needed income.

I think it's time to winterize the mower, Dad announced one morning. We want lawn, not Astroturf.

He and I were tearing down a rotted shed in the backyard with an axe and a sledgehammer. We took a break and drank Crystal Light and admired the destruction. I didn't mention that it would have been more fun to burn it down. Dad did, actually.

You know, he said, wiping his mouth with a glove, that Harvest

Festival is still going on downtown. I'm thinking of taking Mom and your brother tomorrow night. You deserve to come along. How's that sound?

Pretty good, actually.

You used to love the caramel apples.

Yeah, I said.

Finish up that letter for your mom.

I will.

Good. Now hand me that sledgehammer.

Dad borrowed a friend's pickup and we hauled the rotted wood to the dump. I loved the dump. It was enclosed in a gigantic shed. A pair of tractors crawled back and forth over the hills of garbage, VCRs and particleboard furniture and everything else snapping to bits under their treads. Dad backed the truck up to the rim of the concrete canyon and I hopped up into the bed of the pickup with a flathead shovel and pushed everything over the tailgate. All the garbage had a syrupy smell.

The dump felt like a place to start life fresh. To jettison one's baggage and drive away with a lightened load.

When the truck bed was empty, Dad climbed up there with me and we leaned against the cab, staring into that massive concrete hole for a few moments. He didn't take the opportunity to impart wisdom or lecture me, and I appreciated that. There were skylights high above us and all the dust in the air made the sunbeams look like pillars holding the whole place up. It would have been a good time to say sorry.

The Harvest Festival wasn't bad. We wandered among the booths, munching on kettle corn. Fellow festival-goers probably took us for a normal family, which was seventy-five percent true.

After dark, a crowd gathered in a parking lot for a firework show. The explosions blossomed right above us. I watched one ember plummet all the way to the ground, its reflection in the wet parking lot rising to meet it. The colliding comets extinguished one another.

More than once, Todd declared that the finale was awesome, only to be proven wrong by another flourish. Neil Diamond's *America*—with a colorful burst for each exultant *Today!* of the chorus—blended into the typical Tchaikovsky. We stood to hear the *Star-Spangled Banner* sung by a stocky barrel-racing champion on horseback, and for the first time, I really listened to the lyrics. It's a hell of a song. I have since learned that both Mexico and France have anthems about flags soaked in blood, while Germans laud their women, their loyalty, and their wine. We chose to sing about how nice our flag looks all lit up by airborne munitions, which it does.

America, I realized, might be the best place for bomb-worshiping fuckups like me to get a fair shake.

The fireworks did not relent. Patriotic colors burst faster and faster. Then suddenly all was black. The music held steady on a high note. Through the smoke of its predecessors, I happened to notice the ascent of a dark shape. It whistled as it rose, then the whistling stopped.

The quiet lingered.

It lingered.

The explosion, when it came, left no room for debate about the finale. *Humongous* is too terrestrial a word. What we saw was nothing short of a red and white supernova. It seemed to set the slate of the world clean. Seconds later, the BOOM registered against my eardrums and punched me in the guts. Todd and I made many attempts to mimic this noise and this sensation during the car ride home. My ears were still ringing when I got in bed.

I put finishing touches on a lengthier, more remorseful letter, and Mom signed off on it. I sent it to Mr. Weisgard and a few days later he called the house to compliment me on what I'd said, which of course made Mom beam with self-satisfaction. He asked me when I'd be stopping by. I convinced him we should hold off until Christmas vacation, after my debts were paid and I could focus.

That sounds like wisdom, he said. Say hello to your dad.

On Wednesday nights, I went to Boy Scout meetings. I chipped away at the required badges but didn't get much done on my elective badges. In the afternoons after school I rode my bike to Dad's office to file claim documents and man the phones. The financial reconstruction of my life provided precious little time to sulk. Still, while my body worked, my mind obsessed. I began to wonder what the deductible would go toward, specifically. I asked Dad. He said it all went in the same bucket, like taxes, which to me was unacceptable. My hours, my share of the debt, had to pay for a something *specific*, something I could push the mower toward. At some point I came to believe it was the stupid $330 suit.

When I was done Dad looked over my hour tally and saw that I'd I worked 66 hours. Looks like I owe you thirty bucks, mister, he said.

Keep it, I said, walking away pleased. We're even.

TWELVE

For some reason mom was adamant about finishing reconstruction quickly. She said she couldn't fathom hosting the holidays in a wounded house. So, Dad spurred the contractor to work quickly, and by Christmas the house was good as new. Save for a patch of reddish shingles over my room that contrasted with the weathered ones on the rest of the house (and a new skylight Mom wanted over the master bathroom) you couldn't tell we'd had a fire.

We relocated my window though. In my prior room, the bed had been set into the corner, opposite the east window. On summer mornings the slivers of daylight through the blinds were like toaster coils. So when the contractor asked me if I wanted anything different, I requested that the window be moved to the north wall. The room would stay cool and dark, even in the summer. Darkness appealed to me at the time. Other than that, the new room was architecturally identical to the old one, closet and all.

It smelled like fresh paint and wood. The spotless sheetrock at first seemed too vacant, but I didn't want to spend money on posters. The ones I used to have now seemed childish and trite. Before it burned, my room had been a warm den, a place to horde the loot of life. I'd had so much crap on display: a third-place tennis trophy, clever bumper stickers, a topographical map of the moon. Now, I needed a different kind of sanctuary. My new room was perfect. No clutter. No memorabilia. Four white walls, a bed, a desk, and a chair. Sparse as a prison cell.

Weeknights after dinner, I did homework and then rewarded myself with an everlasting shower. I'd sit Indian style on the tile and feel the steam coating my airways. Afterward, I'd shut myself in my room, kill the lights, and collapse face-up on my bed—the Top 9 at 9:00 Countdown piped directly to my soul via headphones. It was all the songs they played at the dances I never went to. I knew all the words.

At Christmas, my aunt and uncle drove up from San Francisco with Grandma Jane. She slept in my room, so I was right back to bunking with Todd.

That Saturday morning, I went out for a walk beyond my usual route. I made a pit stop at Raley's. Whenever I went with Mom to a bookstore I'd always end up finding her in the self-help section; whenever I went in a grocery store, I found myself browsing the cleaning supplies aisle. I'd just gravitate there based on a lack of interest in everything else. On this particular visit, I located a bottle of ammonia but I didn't take it off the shelf. A stocker noticed me.

Help you find something?

Iodine, I said.

Sure. Like for cuts?

I nodded. The stocker looked at me funny. Did he know ammonia and iodine render explosive crystals? Was he on to me? I remembered the time I'd seen Kurt Collins dressed all in black at the checkout counter, buying five dozen eggs.

I skipped the first-aid aisle and bought a Dr. Pepper instead. I was near Mr. Weisgard's neighborhood so I figured I'd aim that direction. Next I knew, I was at his house, knocking on the door. His wife answered. She had on a festive sweater and dangly ornament earrings.

Mr. Weisgard home?

Does he know you?

I'm Oby. He's going to help me with some merit badges.

Right, right. She crossed her arms and looked me over. Everything okay? she asked.

Yes.

She yelled for her husband. While we were waiting together she kept staring at me. Finally, he came to the door. He had gory red stains on his apron and hands, like a coroner interrupted mid-autopsy.

Oby! he said. What'd you hit this time, a reindeer?

Couple.

What a tragedy. Come on in. I'm making cranberry jelly.

Thanks, I said.

I'll introduce you to everyone.

I looked at Mrs. Weisgard. She shrugged. I stepped into the foyer and heard voices in the kitchen.

Quiche just came out of the oven, Mr. Weisgard said. I let it cool on a wire rack to prevent condensation, so the crust stays crisp.

He makes it every year on Christmas Eve, Mrs. Weisgard explained.

I felt like a stray dog who'd wandered onto their porch.

Actually, I said, I think I should go. My family's probably eating, too.

Do they know you're here? Mrs. Weisgard asked.

Of course, they do, darling, Mr. Weisgard said. Oby, let's get cracking on those merit badges soon.

Mrs. Weisgard held the door open. Very nice to meet you, she said. Careful on your bike. It's getting dark.

Merry Christmas, buddy! hollered Mr. Weisgard.

I shut the door before they could see that I didn't have a bike, that I'd covered the distance to their house on foot just to tell Mr. Weisgard…well, nothing.

I ran home. It took me half an hour. The whole family was standing around in the kitchen when I walked in.

Mom saw me first. She spoke my name and came rushing over to clutch me. She felt my forehead. I was still sort of panting. My lungs were dry.

You're roasting! Where in God's name have you been?

On a walk, I said.

All goddamn day? Dad asked.

Your mother's been worried sick, added my uncle. We've been driving around the neighborhood.

I tried calling your friends, Mom said. None of them had any idea where you were. Shane Richardson said you guys don't hang out anymore. Is that true?

I'll go call the Atkinsons, Dad said. Tell them everything's okay.

Sorry, I said. I didn't realize…

Now can we eat? Todd asked.

Everything's cold, honey, Mom said. She threw down her hands and her chin fell to her chest and her head shook as she started to cry, exhausted. My uncle went to hold her.

When at last we were all seated at the table, Dad did his best to catalyze normal conversation. He asked Grandma Jane if my bed had been soft enough for her.

I slept wonderful, she said. Although, for some reason I thought Oby's window used to be on the other wall.

At this, she shook her head and laughed at herself, sucking on a piece of ice from her chardonnay. I looked across the table, trying to snag Mom's attention. Dad was rubbing his hand in circles on her back.

There's more green beans, Mom said, sending the platter around.

On Christmas morning we settled in the living room to open presents. The grownups drank eggnog and Todd and I drank a one-to-one ratio of hot chocolate and marshmallows. We opened gifts one at a time. Dad got me a new Swiss Army knife, its predecessor having melted. My delight was real, although considerably diminished when Todd received the very same knife in the next unwrapping cycle.

Oh, Grandma Jane said, I nearly forgot. She started to get up from the couch. Has anyone seen my purse?

Stay there, Grandma, Mom said. One of the boys will get it.

Todd ran into the kitchen and brought it out and set it on her lap. She fished around to find a pair of envelopes. I opened mine and a $1,000 check fluttered to the floor.

Grandma had always found ways to sprinkle our lives with flavors of a lifestyle just beyond our grasp. Tickets to plays in San Francisco, weekend getaways to wine country. One summer she'd even sent me to an exclusive tennis camp in Florida for three weeks.

Dad shook his head. I think he resented his mother-in-law's charity, especially now that he sort of needed it, and I think Mom did too, but how could they argue?

It was the most money I'd ever held in my hand. The hours I'd put in working off my debt had given me a new appreciation for the value of a dollar, and this check felt like Monopoly money, my due for merely passing Go when really, I belonged in jail.

Maybe you could buy some things to hang in your room, Grandma said. It's rather bare in there.

With this much money I could buy another window, Grandma, I said. For the other wall.

Dad started laughing. Mom punched his arm and glared at me. Grandma adjusted her bracelet and gave a bewildered smile, eggnog on her lip.

THIRTEEN

I didn't ride my bike to Mr. Weisgard's house the day after Christmas, though I considered it. I waited until the day after that. Mrs. Weisgard answered the door in a bathrobe.

Thought you were the milkman, she said. She took an unnerving look at me and a gulp from her coffee mug. You're a very serious boy, aren't you?

Not knowing quite how to respond, I just said, Yes? This seemed to please her. She smiled down at her coffee, then looked up. A moment passed. Finally, she stepped aside and pointed me down the hallway. Her two sons were seated at the kitchen counter in their pajamas, their eyes red with drowsiness. As I took the empty stool between them, they each allowed me a nod—the halfhearted congeniality of bar regulars extended to the obvious tourist.

Oby! Mr. Weisgard said, tending to a skillet of crackling sausage. Sit down. You hungry?

Joyce-Ann held a tattered blanket to her lips and stared at me from behind her dad's leg.

No thank you, I said. I already ate.

Oh yeah? And how old are you, again?

Thirteen.

A plate of steaming scrambled eggs materialized before me.

Then you're hungry, he said.

From the toaster sprung twin toasts. Mr. Weisgard frisbeed one my way. The boys laughed when I fumbled it to the floor. They started counting: *One! Two! Three! Four!* Joyce-Ann jumped up and down, counting along. I climbed down from my stool and joined the count.

Five! I said. I picked up the toast and, to the enjoyment of all, took a massive bite.

Eat up, Mr. Weisgard said. After this, *you're* doing all the cooking.

He is? Joyce-Ann asked.

Mr. Weisgard poured himself more coffee. Yes, honey, he said. In addition to preventing salmonella enteritis and diagramming the food pyramid, Oby here is required by cooking merit badge to prepare three breakfasts, two lunches, and four dinners.

Mr. Weisgard consulted a calendar hanging beside the refrigerator.

Christmas break lasts two weeks, he said. There's four days left this week. Saturday we're visiting some friends in Stockton, back on Sunday, which leaves five days next week. Every time you come over, you're in charge of a meal. That includes planning, shopping, cooking, cleaning. We'll give you some cash for groceries. Consider the kitchen yours. You'll be happy to learn we've got plenty of sodium chloride. Also, we'd prefer if you kept *our* food off the linoleum.

Right, I said.

Mr. Weisgard loaned me his cookbook. It was the coolest cookbook I've ever seen. It more closely resembled a lab notebook, its margins brimming with equations, quick calculations, sketched apparatuses and data from all manner of culinary experiments. (The coolest cookbook I've never seen, by the way, belonged to Marie Curie, whose work discovering polonium and radium left her with radioactive hands that contaminated all she touched, from her lab to her kitchen. Her cookbook is still too dangerous to handle and is kept in a lead box.)

Each day I'd ride my bike to Raley's and buy as much food as I could carry in my backpack. As per Mr. Weisgard's orders, I didn't knock on their front door anymore. I'd lean my bike against their garage and come in through the kitchen. Sometimes, Carbon the cat was the only one who knew I was there until I called everyone to the table.

The Weisgard kids treated me like a foreign exchange student. One time the older boy, Neil, came into the kitchen with two of his friends.

That's him, Neil said, pointing.

I was cooking bacon, a cheap brand, all fat. The splattering oil justified protection. I pulled up my lab goggles and clapped my tongs, a lobster hello.

My brother says you're a pyro, said Neil's friend.

Who's your brother? I asked.

Jim Fitzpatrick. He goes to your school.

Never heard of him, I said, which was true.

Mr. Weisgard came in from the yard, bid us all good morning, and went to the sink to wash his hands. He looked at me in my goggles.

Smart, he said. I barbeque with my fire gloves. Flip steaks by hand.

Mrs. Weisgard wasn't as supportive. She worried I might poison her family. I know this because she told me so. She seemed very curious about me. Suspicious. I was a parolee in her house, among her children. But the longer I stayed, the more we talked and the less she seemed to worry. She showed me her secrets, like how to juggle a yolk in the half shells and how to assure easier cleanups with liberal pretreatments of cooking spray. She loved cooking spray. She used it on knives when cutting dates, she sprayed it on measuring cups to keep honey from sticking, and she sprayed it on vegetables to help seasonings adhere. She did her spraying over the open dishwasher door; that way the counters didn't get greasy.

For my second dinner—roast beef with all the trimmings—Mrs. Weisgard suggested we invite Mom, Dad, and Todd over to share. As we sat down to eat I was treated to a round of applause. Though I'd planned to make a pear tart, Mom had asked if she could be in charge of dessert. After dinner she passed around a plate of oatmeal-raisin cookies. A hush fell over the table as each of us set our teeth against the wafer-thin pucks. Mom hadn't taken one herself. She cringed when Mrs. Weisgard's cookie shattered, raining shrapnel into her lap.

Honey, Dad said, aren't these supposed to be chewier?

Mom was near tears. I know, she said. I don't know what happened. I followed Grandma's recipe exactly.

Where does this grandma live? Mr. Weisgard asked.

San Francisco, I answered. That's where Mom grew up.

Well, there you go, he said. My guess is it's merely a matter of elevation. You've got a sea-level recipe, but Reno's about 4,000 feet higher, and our air is very dry.

You think? Mom said.

Oh, I'm quite sure, Mr. Weisgard said. I've had this problem myself. Water boils at a lower temperature here. And since butter is about twenty-percent water, it melted before your cookies set. All the moisture escaped, so the sugar burned—well, burned a little. He winked.

Mom smiled.

So, what's the fix? Dad asked.

Well, Mr. Weisgard said, I've tried using less butter, which helps. Using less sugar works better. Keeps the dough from spreading too much in the oven. I throw in an extra egg yolk to make the dough chewier. Also, I set the oven about twenty-five degrees hotter and bake for less time so the cookies don't have time to dry out.

Mom had taken a notepad out of her purse and was jotting notes. Dad patted me on the back.

Sounds like Oby's found himself the right teacher, he said.

Mr. Weisgard demurred. Oh, I'm no authority, he said. I've just already made a lot of the common mistakes.

Dad chuckled.

Oby here seems to prefer *uncommon* mistakes, he said.

Every time I stopped at Raley's I bought two bottles of Dr. Pepper. Like the smell of spit that so haunted Dad, the sound of CO_2 hissing from a bottle of Dr. Pepper to this day transports me to Mr. Weisgard's study, our burps punctuating discussion of the chemicals common to toothpaste and Ajax. That's where my second nickname came from: What's the diagnosis, Dr. Pepper? he'd say. Like the time he dropped an iron nail into a beaker of copper sulfate (algae killer from his garage).

What's the diagnosis, Dr. Pepper?

It looks like maybe it's rusting.

There! See? The iron is so reactive it pulls the copper atoms right out of the solution and they stick on the nail.

Is that rusting?

No.

We watched the reaction finish up. Mr. Weisgard burped.

It's like you gave the atoms instructions, I said. They did what you said.

Actually, he said, I have this theory that atoms are female. They do everything on their own terms. But, sometimes, if you massage them just right—set the mood—you can charm them.

I don't know much about girls.

Mr. Weisgard held up the chemistry merit badge booklet. Girls are nothing but atoms, he said.

Interesting, I said. *Interesting* had recently replaced *I know* as my go-to reply. It was a very Spock thing to say. I found it wonderfully versatile: it could be condescending or complimentary, depending on tone.

Mr. Weisgard leaned way back in his chair and crossed his arms behind his head. Of course, he said, a girl is quite certainly more than the sum of her parts. He scribbled some figures on a piece of paper and handed it to me. Some homework, he said.

That night, with the branch of a newly planted hedge tapping against a newly installed window, I calculated that my 148-pound body consisted of approximately 7,000,000,000,000, 000,000,000,000,000 atoms. Suddenly I felt elaborate. How did so many things come to form an Oby? The next day I asked Mr. Weisgard, who shook his head.

The universe is one big recycling program, he said. Some of the atoms in your arm might have belonged to a brontosaurus, and before that, maybe they were part of a volcano. Some were part of your dad, and some your mom. That's a story you ought to hear from them, I think.

On my bike ride home, I thought about what my Dad had been telling me lately—that my troubles would show me what I was made of. Well, now I knew exactly what I was made of. I was a bag of borrowed parts. The next morning at breakfast I asked Mom if she believed in God.

Of course, she said.

Interesting.

Oh, wonderful! So now you're a pyromaniac *and* an atheist?

Never mind, I said. I took a sip of cranapple juice. Mom's eggs were chunky and dense. Did you whisk these? I asked, probing with my fork.

Yes, Oby. I *whisked* them.

FOURTEEN

The line that separates cooking from chemistry was, to Mr. Weisgard, nonexistent. When we couldn't get our hands on a backpacking stove to meet the requirements, we cooked tomato soup and grilled cheese sandwiches on Bunsen burners. Caramelized onions served as a pungent introduction to volatile sulfur compounds. Most of all, Mr. Weisgard cherished the complex chemical reactions of baking. His pantry was kept fully stocked with baking supplies, just in case the mood struck him to whip up some scones, or a cobbler, or focaccia, or brownies, or pizza. He had four types of flour and five types of sugar.

Baking is not jazz, he said. If you vary the recipe, it's to test a hypothesis. It's an experiment. An oven is no place for improvisation.

He showed me his little orange box of baking powder, on which he had written a date.

It's important to minimize variables, he said. Baking powder reacts with acids like buttermilk to make carbon dioxide, which makes dough rise. But the powder can go bad, so you've got to know how old it is. And you've got to test it every so often.

He poured a couple spoonfuls of the powder in a glass of hot tap water and we watched it fizzle and foam.

That's what it's supposed to do, he said.

A few hours later I repeated this test in my own kitchen and ended up with a glass of motionless, chalky water. One small bubble rose and popped. A minute later, a second bubble. Then no more. This of course left me skeptical of the whole kitchen, and of every meal it had ever produced. Following another of Mr. Weisgard's suggestions, I found a dial-face thermometer, put it in the oven, and set the temperature to 400 degrees. While I waited I went to watch *MacGyver*.

Mom came home and asked why the oven was on. I sprung from the couch and ran to the kitchen, stepping past her to open the oven. I peeked at the circular dial. The needle pointed to 360 degrees.

How do we cook in here? I asked.

We? She started laughing.

The oven's not calibrated, I said. The baking powder's dead.

You want to know how *I* cook in here? Mom asked. It's easy: I make food. You and your brother and your father wolf it down. You want to take over? Be my guest!

I'm just saying…

I know exactly what you're saying, young man. And you might want to check your ego while you're checking everything else around here. I'd say it could use some *calibrating*.

I was just trying to help, I muttered, to which Mom scoffed.

I wandered off to call Mr. Weisgard and let him in on my unfortunate discoveries.

Wow, he said. Nicely done. I suppose there's no need to ask if you calibrated your thermometer.

I calibrated the *oven*, I said.

Right, he said. But how do you know your thermometer's not off?

Silence. After a moment Mr. Weisgard said maybe I should check.

Yeah, I muttered. How?

Put it in some boiling water, Mr. Weisgard said. It should read...

Two-hundred-and-twelve.

That's at sea level, remember? It's closer to 204 in Reno. If the reading's wrong, get a pair of your dad's pliers and adjust the nut under the dial until the needle gives the right reading. Don't burn yourself.

But I already had, at least a little. I found the thermometer to be low by 20 degrees, which meant I was half wrong. Mom watched from across the kitchen as I made the prescribed adjustments.

Tuesday night of my second week with the Weisgards I baked them a lasagna. After we ate, Mr. Weisgard and I retreated to the study. He was looking over some of my calculations when Joyce-Anne came in and boosted herself into his lap. Her hair was brushed out and she smelled fresh and shampooed.

Mom said you'd tuck me in.

She did, did she?

And tell me a story.

Mr. Weisgard gave her ribcage a high voltage tickle, during which she arched her back and shrieked with laughter. Mrs. Weisgard yelled from the back of the house.

The idea is to be putting her to sleep!

The three of us looked at each other, straight faced. Joyce-Ann held her breath in her cheeks. Suddenly, Mrs. Weisgard appeared in the doorway to the study and crossed her arms sternly. But we could see she was smiling.

You're here late, she said, looking at me. It's going to be dark before long, mister.

It's *doctor*, Mr. Weisgard said.

Well, I don't want Doctor Oby riding his bike at night. So, when you boys are done, come get me and I'll drive him home.

It's Doctor *Pepper*, darling, Mr. Weisgard said.

My Mom's coming at 8:00, I said, but thank you.

Mrs. Weisgard shook her head and led Joyce-Ann out. The study was quiet again. Mr. Weisgard handed back my calculations. Good, he said. Then he reached below his desk and took out a poster rolled up in a rubber band. He passed it across the desk.

If you're going to be a chemist, he said, or even one of the lesser forms of scientist, you'll need this handy. It's the ingredients to every recipe in the universe.

I worked the band up and off the tube. The periodic table of elements unfurled in my lap.

Really? I said. I studied the poster for a moment. What are these blank squares at the bottom?

Elements that have been predicted, he said, though not officially discovered. Find one of those, you can name it *Obium*. Or *Nevadium*. Just remember who got you started when you win the Nobel Prize.

The Nobel Prize, I said wistfully, re-rolling the poster. Is that in high school?

And so, it was that Mr. Weisgard decided I needed to be told a story just as much as his daughter. More, really. And he made me climb the stairs to Joyce-Ann's room and settle into one of the two undersized chairs at the tea table by the window. Mr. Weisgard sat in the other. At first it was too dark to see much of anything, but soon my eyes adjusted. Stuffed animals littered the rug. Dolls and plastic horses gazed down from the shelves. The room was a crowded theater.

Joyce-Ann squirmed under a polka-dotted bedspread. Mr.

Weisgard rubbed his knees and looked for a moment at the ceiling. He took a deep breath. The room was so quiet that I could hear his tongue peel away from the roof of his mouth…

Alfred Nobel grew up in Sweden, Mr. Weisgard began, so he didn't see much of the sun. During the long nights, he would read by an oil lamp. The lamp gave off a sulfuric, black smoke but Alfred didn't mind. You see, he wanted to be a poet, but his father wanted him to be an inventor.

Alfred studied hard in school, and when he was seventeen he was sent on a boat to America, where he went to work for the man who'd invented a device that pumped warm air to the tops of buildings in New York City. Alfred returned home years later, fluent in five languages, six if you count chemistry, which we will.

He rented an apartment in Stockholm with his brother. One day, Alfred asked his brother to come into the kitchen, which served as their lab. In Alfred's hand was a bottle. He poured out some liquid and hit it with a hammer. The liquid exploded! It was nitroglycerin, see? And Alfred was convinced this new chemical might make him rich.

But the stuff was unpredictable. It exploded when it wasn't supposed to. So he tried mixing it with other ingredients, like black powder. Then he'd go out onto the frozen canals by his house and light the mix with a fuse. He showed his new bomb to some men from the military, but the blast was so big it frightened even them! They actually said it was too dangerous for soldiers—think about that, Oby—too dangerous for war!

Alfred didn't give up. He hired his brother to mix up big batches of nitroglycerin, which they kept in a shed. Well, the shed blew up. No one knows exactly what sparked the blast. When they sifted through the rubble they found five bodies. One of them was Alfred's brother.

Alfred was devastated, and he vowed to make nitroglycerin

safe. How else could his brother's death not be in vain? So he tried new recipes. One time he put in some diatomaceous earth he found along a riverbank. He molded this crazy concoction into sticks and added fuses. He called these sticks *dynamite* and they turned out to be so safe that he carried them around in a suitcase.

Of course, before long Alfred was known as the Dynamite King. He built dynamite factories all over the world. People used the stuff to build roads and dams and all kinds of things. In World War I, one of Alfred's dynamite factories was destroyed by planes dropping dynamite bombs!

But Alfred wanted to make dynamite even more powerful. What he *really* wanted, actually, was to make a substance so devastating that wars would no longer seem like a good solution to anything. He wasn't the first or the last person to think that, by the way, but that's a story for another night.

Anyway, many years after Alfred made his fortune, one of his other brothers grew very sick and died. A French newspaper got confused and accidentally published an obituary about Alfred, calling him a merchant of death and saying he'd made money finding new ways to kill people. Alfred read the story and it haunted him.

In fact, Alfred became so obsessed with how the world would remember him that he rewrote his will. He decided that his fortune should be used to start a fund. And that each year the interest from the fund should be split up and given away as prizes. One prize for the most important contribution to physics. One for chemistry. One for medicine. Since he'd always wanted to be a poet, he said there should be a prize for literature. And one for peace. Later on they added one more, for economics.

Mr. Weisgard glanced over at Joyce-Ann. She was asleep. He finished the story in a whisper.

The Nobel Prizes, he said. You win one of those things, Oby, and *I'll* cook *you* dinner. Unless it's the one for literature.

Deal, I whispered, and he reached across the tea table and we sealed the pact with a firm handshake.

That night when Dr. Pepper got home he went straight to his room. He pushed four thumbtacks into the virgin sheetrock where his window once was and sat in bed gazing at his new alphabet: H, He, Li, Be, C, O...

On the last weekend of Christmas break, Mr. Weisgard invited me along on an outing with his son's Scout troop.

We're celebrating, he said. Four merit badges in two weeks! I've never seen anyone do that.

He wouldn't tell me where we were going, but when I showed up at his house on Sunday morning he was wearing his possum cap. He and I loaded into a pickup with another father, Hank Ambrose, who happened to be a physics teacher.

The only *real* science, Mr. Ambrose assured me. The others are just stamp collecting.

So says Ernest Rutherford, Mr. Weisgard said, nudging me with his elbow. But what did *he* do?

Won the Nobel Prize, Mr. Ambrose said smugly, checking his mirrors as we merged onto I-80.

You're right, he did, Mr. Weisgard said. In *chemistry.*

I got the feeling this wasn't the first time they'd had this little argument. I was sitting in the pickup's middle seat, straddling the stick shift. Mr. Ambrose downshifted to 4th gear and caught me right in the nards.

Whoa! he said. Sorry partner!

Mr. Weisgard patted me on the knee.

Oby here is interested in rapid oxidation, he said.

That so, said Mr. Ambrose, distracted by the traffic. Well then I'd say he's in for a treat today.

There wasn't much conversation the rest of the way. I passed the time by flaring my nostrils whenever the crack in the windshield and the speedometer needle were parallel.

We drove to Dog Valley and parked on a dirt road beside a gully. Mr. Weisgard gathered us all together and handed out little slabs of lead. It was then that I knew what we were up to and I inwardly rejoiced.

He had us verify the softness of the lead with our fingernails before liquefying it in a pot over a campfire. Mr. Ambrose dropped in a gob of beeswax, causing debris trapped in the metal to rise and form a film, which we spooned out into the fire. We took turns pouring the purified lead into a mold and prying it open to release our silvery spheres. Ammo.

Everyone hold out a thumb, Mr. Weisgard said. Line it up so it blocks your view of something in the distance. Now shut your right eye. If your thumb's still lined up with your target, your left eye is your dominant eye. If not, try the other eye. This is how we figure out which shoulder to fire from.

Picture a few dozen boys with dirt mustaches and thumbs raised, sniping unsuspecting signposts and stumps. Our instructions were simple enough, but it would be minutes before those who didn't listen well or couldn't wink or never could do anything on their own finally got it figured out. I was left-eyed. I put down my thumb and waited.

Mr. Weisgard saw me sitting idle and handed me his musket. I nearly dropped it. It was ten times heavier than it looked. The barrel was cool to the touch.

Is it harder if you're left-eyed? I asked. Like being left-handed?

Doesn't matter, Mr. Weisgard said.

What makes you left-eyed or right-eyed?

You, he said.

He did not elaborate. What he did instead was dunk his hand in a bucket of water beside the campfire.

Remember the Leidenfrost effect? he asked.

I nodded. One day in his kitchen, he'd flung some drops of water onto a hot skillet and we'd watched together while they danced around for nearly two minutes, refusing to evaporate. It works, Mr. Weisgard had explained, because a thin film of vapor forms beneath the droplet, insulating it. The hotter the skillet, the longer the droplet dances.

Mr. Weisgard looked around the campfire to be sure no one else was watching us. Then he calmly dipped his wet fingers into the pot of molten lead and just as calmly lifted them back out.

Don't ever do that, he said. But if you do, make sure the lead is at least 400 degrees. Any colder, you'll burn the skin off your fingers.

How'd you know it was 400 degrees? I asked.

I tried it a second ago with a wet hot dog, he said. He winked at me, then called everyone else over.

He put on a demonstration of how to prepare a shot with the rifle. Then we partnered with adults to prepare our own. I feared I was going to blow my hand off with each stroke of the ramrod, packing the ball against the charge, but powder is a patient explosive. It waited for me to put the cap on the nipple, draw a bead on the unsuspecting cardboard deer, exhale.

Mr. Weisgard told us that the barrel ripples in waves from the shock when it fires, and that with muzzleloaders the ignition happens slower than it does with other rifles. So you have to *squeeze* the trigger, nice and slow, because if you jerk it you might flinch from the expected recoil. If the blast doesn't catch you by surprise, say the mountain men, your shot won't be perfect.

K-BOOOOM!!!

Mr. Weisgard and Mr. Ambrose stood peering over my shoulder.

Horrible aim, Mr. Weisgard said.

Maybe I'm right-eyed, I said.

Or blind, he said.

He handed me more ammo. I started packing the charge again. A hiker came down the fire road that led past our makeshift shooting range. He nodded unsurely to Mr. Weisgard and Mr. Ambrose— one of whom was in a possum cap, the other in leather chaps, both watching a boy ramming away at his rod. And written all over the boy's sweaty face: meticulousness. For it was this particular virtue, not listed in the Scout Law, that I most wanted to demonstrate for my mustachioed voyeurs.

I dropped a blasting cap and leaned over to pick it up. Can I still use it if it's got dirt on it? I asked.

Oby, Mr. Weisgard said, Mr. Ambrose and I have been talking. We think you ought to consider an internship of some sort. We'd like to help, of course.

I had a vague idea of what an internship was. My cousin Erin had been an intern in a veterinarian's clinic for a couple summers. Then she went to Creighton to become an anchorwoman and ended up stocking khakis at a mall in Omaha.

You could help a ski patrol blast for avalanches, Mr. Weisgard said. Maybe volunteer for a construction crew. They use explosives. Or help implode old casinos. Nevada's full of things that need blowing up.

Take your pick, Mr. Ambrose said. Matter of fact, I've got a buddy who's a foreman of some sort at a quarry just east of town. I could give him a call. If you like.

Interesting, I said, only half-listening on account of the freshly loaded musket in my arms. I wanted to fire it so I could reload again. I liked reloading better than shooting.

FIFTEEN

The foreman said it wasn't illegal for a 13-year-old to work in the quarry, just stupid. He offered me a job in the office helping the administrative staff, but if I'd wanted to shuffle paperwork I would have gone back to working for Dad.

Call me again when you're in high school, he said.

I really don't see how age figures in here, Mom blurted, immediately covering her mouth. She had promised to let me do the talking.

Excuse me? said the foreman. Is someone else on this line?

That's my mom, I muttered. You're on speakerphone.

Next year Oby is taking a math class at the high school, Mom added. So, *technically...*

All due respect, ma'am, I don't know what kind of mother would want her little boy in a quarry, don't care how smart he is. I'm not just talking about the explosives. My crew, they're hard-working fellas, but they're rough. You got to understand, this is a heavy-duty place.

My grandfather was a steel worker, Mom said. She looked at me and winked, her spirit buoyed by irrefutable blue-collar heredity.

I don't see your point, he said.

Listen, she said, trying a different tack. Oby isn't a little boy. Not anymore.

At this, Mom and I shared a glance which, despite lasting no more than a second or two, seemed to forge the beginning of a new kind of trust, a recognition. For an instant, I saw myself in her, and I wonder if maybe she saw herself in me—the reckless intellect, the devotion to puzzles, be they cardboard or chemical, the deep-seated need to belong, somewhere, anywhere, a quarry, even.

Granted, this glance was fleeting. I started to speak. I wanted to bolster Mom's case by showcasing my maturity, but she put a finger to her lips. The speaker on the phone buzzed softly.

Fine, said the foreman.

And it was agreed that my first day at the quarry would be June 15, 1992—the day after I finished 8th grade, which was over a year away. Once again, I found myself powerless to affect my own situation. It wasn't so much 8th grade that I dreaded. It was the upcoming summer.

Everyone at school pined for the break. But for me, a long sunny day without homework was an explosive mix of idleness and self-loathing that was kept from igniting only by the grace of good air conditioning. School was crappy and mundane, but it *did* move along. It provided a tolerable distraction from myself.

Summer and winter breaks were also the only times of year I lacked a legitimate reason for not hanging out with Kelly. And so, he'd show up out of the blue, on maybe a Tuesday, after breakfast, and ring our doorbell twice, really fast, and I would let Mom go to the door and I'd hear chatting, and Mom laughing.

Oby, she'd call out. Your friend, Kelly, is here!

I'd say nothing.

Kelly had, over the years, come to understand me better than I liked to admit. He preyed on the fact that I no longer had other friends. Often, he'd find me doing something like eating a sandwich or leafing through a magazine, and I wouldn't so much as nod to him. He'd watch without saying a word as I picked up breadcrumbs with my fingertips and helped myself to another handful of chips. I never saw anger in his eyes. He never pouted. He realized that these were the very reactions I sought to evoke. The bastard knew me.

And so what could we do together? Well, first we'd burn up my daily allotment of Nintendo. That summer we played Mega Man 2. I'd be Player 1, die of carelessness in the Metal Man stage, then spend 20 minutes waiting for my life back. Kelly was never casual about Mega Man 2. He determined the sequence of villains he'd battle not just for the weapons he'd obtain in each stage, but the tools. He'd get the jet sled from Air Man before Heat Man's stage, instead of rushing to Wood Man to get the Leaf Shield like I did.

Then two hours would be up and right on cue Mom would waltz in and throw open the curtains, all cheery. She'd tell us it was a gorgeous day. We were wasting it. And we'd yawn and squirm around on the carpet, sunlight pouring in, songbirds mocking us.

Kelly understood that I was under no obligation to play social director. I was happy to mope on the carpet until September. But a salesman can't double-ring a doorbell and expect the person who answers to sell *him* things; Jehovah's Witnesses don't go around *collecting* pamphlets. Clearly, the onus fell on Kelly.

His ideas were clay pigeons, and I wore orange-tinted, sharpshooter sunglasses, my gun shouldered, finger quivering against the trigger, negativity surging through my veins.

We could walk down to 7-11, he'd say.

Lame, I'd say. (Boom! Shattered. Pull...)

Maybe my mom'll drop us off at the mall.

The fucking *mall*?

Wanna go swimming?

Boring. Plus, we have to pay.

I think Kelly knew the certain fate awaiting his first few ideas. I think he tended to save a decent one for when my diminishing well of excuses forced me to be more selective. One day, after sacrificing a few half-hearted ideas, he suggested we play home run derby with crapples. (That's what we called the crab apples in my back yard.)

Maybe, I said, mentally reloading.

You can be up first, he said, sweetening the deal before I could squeeze off another shot.

We swung through the garage to pick up a bat. We had a chest of sports equipment behind the tool bench. Stashed inside among various deflated balls and sprawling cobwebs was a pack of fire-crackers. I recalled a day in the now-so-distant past—the fluttering stomach, the unexpected rising of the garage door.

I grabbed the bat and shut the chest.

Kelly and I gathered all the crapples we could find toward the middle of the yard. We counted them into two piles, making sure we each had the same number of ripe ones (which don't carry very far off the bat) and hard ones. Rules were proposed, debated, rati-fied. The fence running along the east side of the yard became an outfield wall. Cottonwoods became foul poles.

Four hits made an inning. That was the rule. Not four *swings*, we decided (thereby mutually acknowledging, without explicitly stating, that neither of us had stellar hand-eye coordination). And not four *strikes* either. We didn't even have to swing if we thought a pitch was shitty, or if we didn't feel like it. This ensured that pitch-ing would have a minimal impact on the outcome: a crapple home run derby title should be about *hitting*.

I hit only one homer in the first inning. Kelly hit two. But I started grooving my swing in the next inning, and parked my sec-ond and third crapples. I talked trash, only to immediately regret it, not because Kelly retaliated with two homers of his own, but because I'd showed my cards: he knew I was enjoying a game he'd invented.

With Kelly up 4-3, I adjusted my swing to avoid hitting grounders. I would have hit four home runs if the last one hadn't splattered into crapplesauce in midair. I pitched Kelly three of my ripest crapples that inning. I wanted to make sure he wouldn't steal back the lead. This was well within the rules.

By the top of the final inning we were still knotted in a tie. Kelly had hoarded his ripest crapples for this very scenario. Of the four I hit, one broke in half, one was a high pop fly that carried over the wall on a prayer, and two were complete crapplesauce. Fruit flesh caked Kelly's eyebrows, his ears, his hair, his T-shirt. He licked his lips. I handed him the bat. He wiped his palms on the lawn, took a few practice cuts, and sidled into the garden-hose batter's box. I tossed him one and he swatted it farther than any we'd hit all day.

So, I started throwing junk. Both of us knew it. Kelly watched five in a row go by.

Seriously? he said.

I'm *trying*, I said.

Kelly got impatient and on the next pitch his eyes got wide and he swung too early, fouling the crapple into the neighbor's yard. Which left two crapples. He needed one homer to win. I had one hard, little crapple and one big, juicy one. I decided to try the hard one first, even giving Kelly a decent pitch. But he had, by then, become so inured to bad pitches that he didn't even swing.

What was wrong with *that*? I asked self-righteously, knowing my one good pitch had undermined Kelly's right to complain, that I'd bought myself five horrible pitches.

Go, he said, tossing the small crapple back to me. He dug his feet in and gnawed his lower lip. The top of his bat traced anxious little orbits.

I tossed the crapple kind of hard and he caught it out front.

It made a popping noise on the bat and took off toward left field. Crapples don't fly all that true. It curved and struck the left-field cottonwood.

I held my arm out like an ump. Foul!

Fuck, Kelly said.

One more, I said. I held it up so he could see the worm holes, the bruises.

You can kiss it goodbye, he said.

You can kiss my bonch, I replied.

I pitched it nice and easy, but with a hint of topspin. He swung as if to murder it. I didn't so much see the crapple as sense it. It was most of the way to my head by the time I thought to dodge it. I managed to turn a couple degrees, then it exploded against the side of my face.

The first thing was, my ear started ringing. Then the crapple-sauce started to sting my eye and tears welled up. My face began to swell and throb. I touched my cheek tentatively, pulling away chunks of crapple skin and seeds. I could see a blur shaped like Kelly, using the bat like a cane to hold itself upright.

That's how hard the blur was laughing.

Something in me ignited. I could taste the overripe fruit and the faint, metallic tint of blood. Moving with quickness I'd never known, I got from the pitcher's mound to the batter's box in an instant and pounced. I pinned Kelly's face in the grass. I kneed him in the ribs. I rained down punches, striking anywhere I found an opening. I saw red.

Keep laughing, shitface! Keep laughing!

Ow! Fucker! Ow, Jesus!

I held back a little to see if he'd retaliate but he kept whelping and flinching, which only aroused my tantrum. I felt levels of rage usually only Todd could conjure. Kelly made futile kicks at my shins. I was a barrage of elbows, knees, knuckles, heels.

Eventually, Kelly gained leverage. He took hold of my wrists and butted his head against the bridge of my nose and the pain was so sharp I relented and before I knew it he'd flipped me on my back and jammed his forearm into my Adam's apple. With his face so close, I could see his nostrils flaring in and out. Bits of dirt and spittle were stuck to the corners of his mouth. He had me pinned. I caught my breath. He caught his. It was a momentary, unspoken truce. Then Kelly tilted his head and his open lips came down and sealed against mine.

SIXTEEN

At which point, Kelly got all nonchalant. I squirmed free, put some lawn between us. I couldn't even look at him.

I thought you'd be into it, Kelly said. I thought you were mature.

He was on his back, legs crossed at the ankles, as if he was just chatting with the clouds.

You idiot! I said. What if someone saw? What if my Mom just saw that?

He sat up and shook his head dismissively, all calm. Me, I couldn't keep my hands still. I threw a chunk of bark.

Have you ever kissed a girl, Oby? I never see you at any of the dances. Or the parties.

Leave.

Amanda and those girls think you're a homo.

Leave! Wait, did they say that?

Well, aren't you?

I thought you were my friend, I said.

Is that why you treat me like shit, then? I'm not *stupid*, Oby.

Kelly turned away. I was dying to pin him on his back like a turtle again. I wanted to get back to being the one metering out mercy.

Have you done this before? I asked. With other guys?

Kelly tugged out some grass.

Tell me! I said.

Kelly just nodded. And despite further prodding, he refused to tell me who the others had been.

Somehow, knowing I wasn't Kelly's first pissed me off. His wasn't some misguided crush. He seemed so sure, laser-guided. He had an assassin's patience, and my name was one on a growing list of conquests. By comparison, my own lusts felt volatile and aimless, closer to rage than romance. Sometimes at school, it was all I could do just to keep from swerving down the hall with my arms out, frenching drinking fountains, dry humping lockers. Of course, other times I felt like an androgynous bulge of lukewarm mashed potatoes. In a single hour, I'd go from bored to confused to lonely to desperate to masturbating and back to bored again.

I heard Mom's voice. She was on the back porch, offering tuna sandwiches.

No thank you, Mrs. Brooks! Kelly hollered. I have a dentist appointment!

With that, he looked me straight in the eye, got up, and walked out of the yard.

I stayed on the grass for a while, I couldn't say how long. When I finally went inside I lay on the floor of my room, watching a bug struggling around inside the dome lamp on my ceiling.

Kelly had tainted me. I'd never kissed a girl, it was true. I'd never kissed anyone. Kelly knew me. It was something I'd postponed, like so many other inevitabilities. I was a guy; eventually

I'd get around to girls, right? After I won the Nobel Prize, maybe. After my speech. I'd be wearing a tuxedo. She'd be all clingy, awed by my contribution to science. She'd have great boobs. Milk-white, antigravity, heiress boobs, big as dome lamps.

Now, however, if my sexual history were being kept in a file somewhere, and if that file were to come under review, the rubber stamp would be swift. I was 100 percent, USDA Choice homo until I made out with a girl, at which point I'd be 50/50 and the review panel would have to take into account new variables: duration of encounter, willingness of participants, tongue, et cetera. Still, even if I had an orgy with Amanda and her friends every day for the rest of the summer, or hell, the rest of my life, I was always going to be gay to some decimal point. And so what? Hetero/homo—did I even give a shit either way? My friends were heteros, but I hated my friends. I didn't have friends, except Kelly.

Was there such a thing as pyrosexual?

———————————

The next morning, I stayed in bed and brooded. Kelly surely knew I wasn't going to tell anyone, but would he? What would I say in my own defense? That the school pussy had his way with me? The kiss seemed to linger on my lips, the bitter taste of crapplesauce and sweat. I could still see the shadow of Kelly's head as it eclipsed the afternoon sun.

I heard Mom, Dad, and Todd chatting at the breakfast table before Dad left for work. When at last the kitchen was quiet I slipped down the hallway and toasted myself a pair of Eggos. I buttered and ate them like toast while staring out the window over the sink. Then I retreated to my room and slipped back under the covers. I tried to fall asleep but tensely anticipated the doorbell. Todd knocked to see if I wanted to play Nintendo. I shooed him.

Mom came in and felt my forehead. You're burning up, she said.

I'm *fine*. I'm just a little tired.

Interesting, she said. *Very*, I thought. Wasn't interesting *my* word? Or had it been hers all along? Like the time I heard "Born in the U.S.A." on the radio and asked Dad to take me to the mall so I could buy the tape, only to hear him laugh as he showed me the four Springsteen albums already in our record cabinet.

To prove to her I didn't need attention, and to myself I didn't have mono, I jogged down to 7-Eleven, going four blocks out of my way to avoid Kelly's house. I bought a Dr. Pepper, drank it on the curb, and walked home. When I got back Mom was trimming deadheads off the marigolds in the front yard. I asked her for some money to go to the pool. Maybe, I'd get lucky and drown. From what I'd heard it was like falling asleep.

You have your own money, Oby. She wiped her brow with her forearm. Who you going with?

Mom would never let me go to the pool alone. Sadly, there was only one name I could give that wouldn't arouse suspicion, no matter how bitter the taste it left as I spoke it.

I rode my bike to the river and sat on a rock. A family with two little boys drifted by on an inflatable raft. The mother pointed me out and they waved as though I were a character on a Disneyland ride, some effeminate turtle at water's edge with a clever chorus about hard times and thick shells. It was plain to see that this family believed everyone they came across was just as happy about things as they were. I became paranoid about Kelly calling the house and spoiling my alibi, so I rode home full speed, only to meet Dad in the driveway. He'd just gotten home from work.

I forgot to thank you for picking up the crab apples, he said. It's nice to see you taking some initiative.

The next day, Todd and I played *Mega Man 2* for four and a half hours while Mom ran errands. Kelly didn't call. He didn't call for a week. Then one morning as I was stepping into the shower (just to pass some of the time until lunch) the doorbell rang and I became acutely aware of my own heartbeat. I put my clothes back on as fast as I could and eavesdropped from my room. Kelly's voice. Mom's laughter. I decided that I couldn't just wait for Kelly to come and trap me alone in my room. I had no choice but to walk down the hall and face him in the foyer. When he saw me he gave a little nod.

All right then, Mom said. I'll leave you two alone.

She patted her hand on Kelly's shoulder and walked away. He and I stood there for a minute.

Want to go to a movie? I said.

I saw him hesitate: here *I* was, lobbing an idea through *his* crosshairs. Here was his inaugural chance to shoot me down.

Okay, he said.

Mom drove us to the theater. While we were standing in line for tickets, a pair of bums hovered near the dumpster. The way they stared at us, it was as though they knew what we'd done. Their red eyes saw straight through us. Finally, we were inside the theater and out of sight. We sat side by side, rocking anxiously in the creaking seats.

Did you tell anyone? I whispered.

Everyone.

I'm serious, Kelly.

Who would I tell? Nobody cares what you do.

It's bad enough people think I'm some kind of pyro.

Oby, you *are* some kind of pyro.

I started to argue but the house lights dimmed and Kelly shushed me. Don't worry, he said, popping a Hot Tamale in his mouth. I think it's kind of cool, actually.

Kelly's words ricocheted inside my head as we sat together in silence and watched *Terminator 2*. The theater was dark and cool and I was content with my thoughts. I was entertained. Then the credits rolled and we reemerged into the harsh daylight and sweltering blacktop of the parking lot.

Something needed happening. July became August. The days began to bore me in a way regular people could never fathom. Life was a slow-burning fuse with nothing at the end. I spent most of my time at home by myself. The second hand on the kitchen clock whittled away at the days and weeks until school started. At the end of most days I had nothing to show for having lived except shampooed hair.

The tedium was exacerbated by a medium-strength migraine that arrived one Friday afternoon. Dad came home from work to find me in bed and he went out to the kitchen and grabbed the fire extinguisher from under the sink and brought it to my room and, without saying a word, set it at the foot of my bed.

Ha, ha, I said.

The migraine progressed to regular-strength overnight and I spent Saturday morning on the couch with an icepack over my face, acutely aware of my pulse. Time came to a near-standstill. Todd and my parents kindly tiptoed around me, going about their regular-paced lives.

A few days later Kelly came over with a pipe and a bag of pot. We went back to his house and smoked, solemn as Indian chiefs. That summer we smoked quite a few pipe loads behind Kelly's garage. Both of us had all our chips on the table. He knew I was a pyromaniac loser and I knew he was a predatory lover. We could speak frankly. We could get high without fear of revealing too much of ourselves. Each of us queer in his own way, Kelly and I finally talked straight.

I want to win the Nobel Prize, I told him one afternoon.

I want a pizza, he replied, with tons of olives.

I funded our habit with my grandma's Christmas money. Since we weren't in school, Kelly had a tough time arranging ways to sneak off and buy more pot, or if we did manage to get a little, we sometimes had to wait a few days for Kelly's mom and his sisters to leave the house long enough for us to smoke it. We didn't want to smoke anywhere else for fear we'd be caught. At Kelly's house, we could control the circumstances. Once I got the hang of holding the smoke in my lungs, being high helped me forget myself. Best of all, its effects lingered into the afternoon and evening. It meant I didn't have to ride a bike or swim or do anything, really, to get tired, so I could go to sleep. Pot was a gateway. Sleep was the ultimate high.

And I would have made a respectable stoner if 8th grade hadn't intervened. Word problems and reading assignments ebbed back into the hollow places in my life. I welcomed the essays, over-studied for the exams. Kelly eventually stopped following me home. Summer was over and now he was the one with other friends—a whole crew of drama queens and kings who wore tight pants and unashamedly belted out Broadway musicals in public.

So, Kelly and I would step off the bus together each afternoon and stand for a moment on the side of the road. The air brakes would disengage with a hiss and through a lingering haze of dust and exhaust we'd flash blasé peace signs and turn our separate ways. Mom stopped stocking Vienna sausage.

I didn't make much of it, probably because there was never an official parting of the ways. Over the years, he'd gone from nag to attacker to enabler and, eventually, to equal. While I'd never truly liked him, I had come to respect him. He didn't care much for what others thought, and this was something I noticed, though it was lost on me until much later. He and I, we simply drifted apart, drawn to separate poles. It's impossible for boys to know at the time that a given blasé exchange of peace signs is to be their last.

Without spare time to dwell on how crappy everything was, time flew by. It was Halloween. Christmas. Then came the long, cold months before the foothills turned green again. I finally understood the way normal kids felt about summer. Now it couldn't come fast enough. Each fickle dip of the thermometer depressed me. In June, I called the quarry to confirm I still had an internship, that they hadn't reconsidered their ludicrous offer to teach a teenaged boy how to blow things up. They gave me the same answer they'd given the first time I'd called, back in May: Yes, I still had the job, and please don't call again.

They had no idea how unbalanced the equation was, how disproportionate my need for them was compared to their need for me. I think my desire had a little to do with making Mr. Weisgard proud, a little to do with proving to my parents I could be worth something, and a lot to do with not wanting to feel like a victim anymore.

I'd recently had a weird dream in which MacGyver appeared as a guest on *Sally Jesse Raphael*, but instead of being all strong and collected, he was a mess. He whined about his father and a desire to settle down, to find a wife. At one point, Sally Jesse handed him a tissue. I'm no interpreter of dreams, but this one was concerning. Was I that spineless? Did mere exposure to my subconscious shrivel even fictional badasses?

The hills around Reno yellowed. The air turned hot and dry. Afternoon thunderstorms sent more lightning to the ground than rain. Brushfires flared up, blackening mountainsides. Atoms that had been sagebrush and pine trees were reincarnated as smoke. I rubbed my itching eyes.

At last, something was happening.

SEVENTEEN

It was thirty minutes to the quarry by wood-paneled Wagoneer. Mom drove me out there for the first time on June 15, 1992, the day after I graduated from 8th grade. A Monday. Partly cloudy. Now, officially a high school freshman, I had the world-at-large's implicit endorsement to handle explosives semi-professionally. Mom made my lunch. She also insisted I wear a tie. First impressions, she said.

East of Reno, Interstate 80 parallels the Truckee River, winding its way into the desert. Very few tourists drive into the middle of Nevada on a given Monday morning. The traffic consists mainly of semis and pickups, ranchers commuting to towns like Elko, Fernley, Fallon. That morning, the Wagoneer was what Mr. Weisgard would have called an *outlier in the data*.

It's a lonely stretch of highway. I'd heard the Mustang Ranch whorehouse was out there somewhere, though I never saw it. Truckers peering down from their cabins at Mom and me might very well have guessed we were on our way to Salt Lake City: I was, after all, suitably dressed for choir tryouts at the Mormon Tabernacle.

Hot morning sunlight beat through the windshield. I broke out in post-shower perspiration. Mom turned on the AC. My sweats turned to chills.

This is the exit, I said. There weren't any houses or buildings in sight. A couple of truckers had parked on a patch of gravel beside the off-ramp, probably catching naps before the long haul across no man's land. We turned away from the river and climbed into the foothills.

I began to second guess my navigational skills, as did Mom, and popped open the glove compartment to fetch the map. I unfolded it and rediscovered the iterative scrawling of my former self—the one who'd not so long ago sat idly in Mr. Weisgard's driveway, practicing his signature all over the Great Basin. How had I changed since that day?

How hadn't I?

A Ford Ranger pickup approached us from the opposite direction. It was the first sign of life we'd seen since turning away from the interstate, and as it passed I glimpsed a peeling quarry logo on its door. The road was bendy, so we couldn't see too far ahead. We'd gone at least five miles when we spotted a wood post bearing a sign no bigger than a license plate with the quarry's name on it. Mom slammed on the brakes in time to make the turn. Pavement gave way to gravel. We followed a set of high-voltage power lines up a slight grade, toward a massive hole in the side of a mountain. Like the flesh of a bitten apple, the exposed soil of the hole had turned a darker shade of brown.

Was I anxious about my new job? Yes and no. I liken my state of mind that day to that of a samurai. To become fearless warriors, the samurai imagine they are dead already, and so have nothing to lose. For me, this took little imagination.

The further we drove, the worse the road. We bounced across ruts caused by erosion. All of a sudden Mom pulled off to the shoulder.

What? I asked, and she pointed at a dump truck the size of a McDonald's lumbering toward us. The tires were taller than the Wagoneer. We stared up at the driver as he roared by, but he didn't so much as nod to us, leaving us to wonder, as Mom pulled back onto the road, if we might soon pass the pancaked remnants of those who'd failed to yield. I kept my eye out the back window, watching the truck recede into a dust storm of its own creation.

Further up, we came to a complex of squatty buildings and dusty trailers. There weren't any marked parking spaces in the dirt lot. The cars and trucks were parked at random; meanwhile, the squadron of Harleys along the chain link fence formed a neat row, all the bikes leaning at the same kickstand angle. Mom found some space near an old shed and turned off the engine.

What are you doing? I asked.

I'm coming in.

Wait, why?

She got out and shut the door. I got out, too. The temperature was already into the 80s. Nearby air conditioning units hummed steadily. I followed Mom toward what looked like the main office, a two-story concrete box with tinted windows and a pair of flag poles out front. Mom held the door open for me. Inside, the air was almost cold.

The receptionist looked surprised to see us, to see anyone.

We weren't sure where to go, Mom said. My son is reporting for an internship.

The receptionist picked up a radio.

Bill, this is Maggie, over.

We waited for the radio to squawk to life. Maggie took a drag from a Super Big Gulp. Eventually, someone answered.

Go ahead, Maggie.

What's your 20, Bill?

Section D.

I have a boy and his mother here to see you.

For a few moments, there was silence on Bill's end. We waited again.

10-4, he grumbled. We're all but done loading the Henderson order. Be there in fifteen, over.

Creeping in behind Bill's voice were all kinds of noises—the beeping of a truck, big machinery, men yelling, radio static. A veritable war zone.

Copy that, Maggie said.

She set the walkie-talkie back in its charger and motioned to a pair of chairs that constituted the waiting room. She offered us coffee. Mom declined for both of us. I wandered over to a framed map of the quarry. It showed property lines, topographic features, and all sorts of intriguing colored symbols. I studied this map intently. I felt compelled to memorize it, or at least appear inquisitive. First impressions.

Oby, come sit down, Mom said, meanwhile reapplying lipstick in her compact mirror.

The receptionist loaded a form into a typewriter, pecked a few strokes, resituated the paper. She pretended not to watch as Mom reached up from her chair with both hands and cinched my half-Windsor snuggly against my Adam's apple.

You could use a haircut, she said.

I stood up again, afraid Mom might lick her thumb and rub dried milk off my cheeks.

Actually Maggie, I said, I'll take some coffee.

Mom looked at me like I'd pissed my khakis.

I drank it at tennis camp, I said, carefree as a billionaire.

I would very soon come to regret this admonition, though I

never did get any coffee because the main door opened and a gust of hot wind rustled the papers on Maggie's desk, and in walked Bill. He wore a hard hat and work boots. In the back pocket of his Wrangler jeans, a wallet impression; in the breast pocket of his faded polo, a crumpled pack of Marlboros. He wiped his palm across his shirt before shaking our hands, first Mom's then mine. His eyes were bloodshot. Cordial, though gruff, he complimented my professional attire.

Mom lifted her chin, beholding me. Doesn't he look great? she said. She smoothed back my hair and kissed me on the forehead.

Yes, ma'am, Bill said.

With a smile to Maggie, Mom shouldered her purse and readied herself to go.

Oh, she said. What time do I pick Oby up?

Five o'clock sharp, Bill said.

Of course, Mom said. Just like a real job.

Bill disappeared down a narrow hallway. I hustled to catch up. We passed a little kitchen and some offices where people were working and arrived in a conference room. Bill cleared a set of blueprints off the table.

God damn it, he said. Run and see if your mom already drove off, would you? I need her signature on this liability form.

I hesitated momentarily.

Now!

Oh!

So, out the door and down the hall I ran, back through the lobby and out into the hot parking lot in time to see the Wagoneer turning onto the empty dirt road. Mom had her turn signal on. I gave chase, tie tailing over my shoulder, topsiders gaining little purchase on the loose gravel, arms waving like tentacles.

Mom! Mom!

After about 50 yards of fruitless sprinting and yelling I slowed to a jog, then a walk, and finally a halt. Tributaries of sweat and hair spray trickled down my neck. I unbuttoned my collar, loosened my tie. My first quarry mission, and I had failed.

I guess today you're stuck doing desk work, Bill said when I got back.

That's fine, I said. Whatever's fine.

Hell, at least you're dressed for it.

A crackly, disembodied voice came over the radio asking a question loaded with urgency and alphanumeric lingo.

Jesus Christ, said Bill. He tapped the pack of Marlboros against his forearm and took out a cigarette. He stuck it behind his ear and started to replace the pack in his breast pocket before, almost apologetically, holding it out for me.

No, thanks, I said.

You're not a dipshit are you, kid?

No, I said.

Good. We've got more than we can handle around here already. He slid a stack of paperwork across the table. Fill this out, he said. Your liability form ain't signed yet, so don't get a paper cut and sue me.

A tall man in tight jeans came into the conference room. Bill handed him a roll of blueprints. The man had a mustache on his top lip and a plug of tobacco in the bottom.

Who we got here? he said.

This is Oby, Bill said. Oby, this is Jack.

I stopped filling out forms and shook Jack's hand, squeezing at about 80 percent of my absolute hardest.

Nice tie, kid. Maggie tells me you play tennis.

What? I stammered. Oh—well, I went to camp once is all. You play?

He and Bill shared a look.

Jack's a driller, Bill said, as if that were some kind of explanation. You probably won't be working much with him. At least not right away.

Jack moseyed over to the water cooler in the corner of the room. He drank the first cup in one gulp and started to refill it.

Who's Oby going to be working for? he asked.

Terry, Bill said, almost in a whisper.

A bubble glugged inside the water cooler. Jack grinned. He put the little cup to his lips once more and tilted his head back, grimacing as if the water were whiskey, a final shot at the bar before saddling back up. Completing the image, he wiped his mustache with his shirtsleeve. Then he crumpled the cup in his fist and let it fall in the trash.

On his way out the door, Jack slapped me on the back at what I suspect was about 40 percent of his hardest. I clenched my jaw and waited for the stinging to subside, doing my best to sit still. Bill nodded to Jack. Be right out, he said. Then Jack was gone.

Who's Terry? I said.

Your new boss.

Do I meet him today?

Bill chuckled.

EIGHTEEN

Turns out it was *Teri*, not *Terry*, and that *he* was in fact a *she*. During the summer I spent in her charge, I never learned her official title. I'm pretty sure she didn't have one. Her duties were too nebulous. Mr. Weisgard once explained antimatter to me. No one can see it, he'd said, but they say it makes up most of the universe. Without it, all the equations don't balance and the universe isn't possible. I hadn't fully understood what he meant, but then I met Teri. Teri was The Anti-Quarry. That should have been her title.

All the other women who worked at the quarry spent most of their time safely behind desks, or on the phone, rarely venturing into the quarry proper. Teri was a different species. Certain bacteria manage to thrive inside sulfuric volcano vents on the ocean floor. Teri chose the quarry, with its toxic concentrations of testosterone. She served as liaison among the drillers and the muckers, the accountants and the engineers, the women and the men. She didn't seem to take orders from anyone in particular, from anyone at all, really. Her Ford Ranger glided through the quarry as the Popemobile through Mexico City: white, bulletproof, sacred. People came to her with problems. She put out fires. She wore Old Spice.

Over the radio, Teri's voice was both sing-songy and hoarse.

I have the new kid here with me, Bill told her.

Preppy?

Oby, actually. Boy's name is Oby.

That's not what I heard.

I learned that day just how fast word traveled at the quarry. Faster than the compression waves that once a week ripped new holes in the mountain. Faster, even, than rumors at a middle school.

Bill walked me out the door of the main building. Standing together on the front steps, he pointed to the far side of the parking lot.

See that trailer on blocks over there? he said.

The one all by itself?

That's the one. That's Teri's office. I advise knocking.

And with a brisk slap on the back, he set me in motion. It was the second time my back had been slapped that day, but this time I appreciated the impetus. Teri's trailer had the haunting look of an abandoned stagecoach, an anachronism in the landscape. The desert whipped dust in my eyes as I crossed the lot. The heat came up through the soles of my topsiders. I arrived at the metal step that protruded from below her trailer door. I wiped my feet on a welcome mat and followed Bill's one bit of advice.

Someone inside yelled something. I waited for a moment, then took hold of the undersized, spring-loaded knob and turned gently, only to have the wind suddenly snatch the door out of my hands. It banged against the outer shell of the trailer. I got hold of the door and stepped inside, apologizing as I wrestled the door back into its latch.

The air in the trailer was cold. Teri kept her air conditioner on full blast. She hated the heat, I came to learn. She also hated dirt, in general. And meat, she hated meat, which was how she got her name—the minimally syllabic drillers having somehow truncated 'vegetarian' to 'Teri.' Teri hated lots of things, but the more I learned about her, the more I came to see that these same things were vital to her. She *loved* to hate them. Daily contact with these things honed her edges. The quarry was nothing without her and she was nothing without the quarry. She loathed the quarry.

I scanned the trailer's cramped interior but couldn't see anyone. Filing cabinets lined one wall. At the far end was a couch and beside it a table. Greasy machine parts had been meticulously arranged on the table, oriented properly with respect to each other, a puzzle solved but not assembled. I looked around some more, saw a microwave, a fridge, potted plants blooming in the windowsills, strange crystals and rocks on the shelves, and maps of the quarry tacked to wood paneling.

Teri surprised me from behind, materializing through a door at the back of the trailer, one she shut as soon as she came through. She offered her hand. I gripped it and shook. The way she looked at me I felt as though I'd passed a test. With a C-.

She wore a purple T-shirt and jeans and had naturally curly hair that hung almost to her shoulders. Sunglasses had left tan lines on the bridge of her nose and across her temples. She wore work boots, although they were daintier than I'd expected—with light blue accents and tassels near the toe. But I wasn't the only one taking stock of footwear.

Thought we'd be sailing today? Teri asked.

Oh, I said, glancing down at my Sperrys. My mom thought...

She still dressing you?

Teri talked in questions, especially when addressing those of us forever lacking answers.

I can change, I said.

You better.

But, really, I couldn't change. I hadn't brought anything else to wear. And I couldn't do any real work, the type that necessitated the liability waver, until Mom signed it. The best I could manage was to take off my button-down shirt, leaving just my gray undershirt.

You can ride in a truck, can't you, Preppy?

Teri grabbed her keys, a thermos, and a hat. It was a cowboy hat with a small brim. More Crocodile Dundee than John Wayne, encircled by a sweat-stained turquoise bandana. We drove out to the quarry road then turned left onto the asphalt. Teri rolled down her window. Wind swirled inside the cabin. Papers from the backseat blew into my lap. Teri checked her mirrors and drove on, holding her chin up and filling her lungs with the fresh air. I thought it wise to keep my mouth shut.

No pouting, she said.

I'm not.

I know, she said. It's not an order, it's a rule. You meet Arnie yet?

Um…

Doesn't matter. Arnie's one of our drillers. His wife, Loni— she's been calling the quarry since back in May, hassling the secretaries and complaining about all the blasting. Says it feels like an earthquake at her house. Hell of an embarrassment for poor old Arnie. But Loni doesn't like living out here in the middle of nowhere. It's not for everyone, I'll give her that. And she doesn't like Arnie working at the quarry. Probably doesn't like Arnie.

I smiled. Teri noticed.

Anyway, she continued, about a month ago I drove out to see

Loni. Set up a CSM to see how much we're making their place shake. This woman's crazy enough to sue us, even if Arnie's still on staff. So, I felt I needed some hard data.

CSM? I asked.

Continuous seismic meter, I'm pretty sure. Or maybe the M is for monitor? *Shit*, who cares! Last week I came out here and picked it up. Looked at the tape and, sure enough, every Friday around 1:00 when we do our shot there's a decent sized blip and a little chatter afterward on account of the fallout. But some other spikes too, bigger ones that seem to show up every Monday close to noon. Those can't be from the quarry. And there's no train track out here or anything. Since today's Monday, I thought I'd head out and see what all the commotion is.

Interesting, I said.

She looked away from the road at me, like I'd said something amusing. *Very*, she said.

We drove another mile or so. Teri pulled off the road at a bashed-in mailbox on a leaning pipe, the base of which rose from a misshapen lump of concrete. The house was missing paint in many places and missing quite a few shingles. Tires had worn twin tracks through the weeds. A ripped screen door flapped in the breeze.

Aha! Teri said. She stopped the truck. See over there, she said, on the side of the house by the power pole? That's where I set up the CSM.

By that Harley?

That's a Honda, kid.

Oh.

Reason it matters is, all the drillers, Arnie included, ride Harleys.

Teri turned the truck around and we started back down the road to the quarry.

So, whose Honda was that? I asked.

Teri shrugged. Hell if I know, she said. What I do know is, next time that cheating bitch calls to complain, I'll be happy to tell her what else is rocking her house. How's *that* for interesting?

I smiled to be in on such a scandalous secret. So, you're not going to tell Arnie? I said.

Not really my business. So, no. And neither are you.

She looked across the bench seat, reading the level of commitment in my eyes. Satisfied, she returned her attention to the road and started shaking her head.

People, she muttered. As if the designation did not apply to her. To *us*.

I couldn't have agreed more, Teri. Fucking *people*.

NINETEEN

The next morning, I got out of the Wagoneer before Mom could kiss me goodbye. I was early. None of the Harleys were there yet. I knocked on Teri's trailer.

That you, Preppy?

I hesitated. Clearly, answering to such slander was to consent to it, but what choice did I have? Yeah, I sighed.

I'm out back.

I circled around the side of the trailer to find Teri sitting in a rope hammock, her toes providing little pushes. The hammock was suspended from bolts drilled into a pair of boulders which, upon closer inspection, I realized were in fact one massive boulder that had cracked in half. Painted on one of the halves was the word *rock*. *Hard place* was on the other. Teri's back was to the trailer. She looked out over the desert, cool and orange.

I didn't know this was back here, I said.

You got the waiver? she said.

I held it out. Swoops of green calligraphy had bled through the form, Mom's signature visible on both sides. Asking Mom to sign it had felt criminal. Did she not realize she was granting me the right to handle explosives with complete impunity? Of course, legitimacy was the only option I had left. I'd very much blown my cover with the covert stuff.

Okay then, Teri said. Let's go out to the stable.

That's what she called the five-bay garage, a shoe-box-shaped building wrapped in corrugated aluminum. Inside, tools hung along the walls in neat rows. The concrete floor was swept and spotless, save for a few grease stains. Four of the bays were occupied by '84 Ford Ranger pickups, each painted white with a big quarry logo on the door and a toolbox mounted behind the cabin.

I want them clean, Teri said, inside and out. The crew has a meeting this morning, but they'll need the trucks after lunch.

She grabbed a bucket and some soap out of a closet and lay a stack of red rags over my forearm so I looked like a waiter.

Bring the trucks out here by the hose to wash them, she said. Gas them up while you're at it. There's a pump around the other side. Do your drying before the dust sticks, then pull them back inside and give them a good vacuuming.

She pointed out the Shop-Vac in the corner of the garage. Two of its four caster wheels were missing, I soon learned, which meant that in order to move it I had to squat down, bear hug it, then straighten up and waddle to where I needed it, the hose trailing over my shoulder like I was kidnapping a baby elephant. Teri handed me four key rings and walked away, already barking into her radio. I dared not interrupt, though it seemed worth mentioning that I'd never driven a car. But I figured I'd watched the Wagoneer driven enough to get the idea. So I didn't bring it up. Nor did I ask when I might get my hands on some boosters. I was already wise enough to know that these weren't the kinds of questions Teri liked, or answered.

But as soon as she was gone I came to discover that the Rangers were all equipped with a second brake pedal. I didn't know how it worked so I had to track Teri down. I led her over to the open driver door.

That? she laughed, looking to where I was pointing. The clutch?

She taught me the basics in about an hour. We pulled one of the trucks out of the garage and practiced in the dirt lot. There was a lot of stalling and stuttering and over-revving to begin with, but I soon acquired a feel for the pedals and the little dance move that engaged the gears. *Squeeze the trigger, don't pull,* I thought. We practiced first gear and reverse since those were all I'd need to get a truck washed. I worked the clutch so many times that my left leg was a little stiff when I got into bed that night. Similar lessons would continue throughout the summer. On the rutted dirt back roads of Sections F and G, Teri taught me how to drive like a man, how to steer into a skid, how to use my gears like brakes. I didn't tell Mom and Dad because I didn't want Teri to get in trouble. Dad later enjoyed a false satisfaction when, under what he believed to be his tutelage, I parallel parked the wood-paneled Wagoneer like a veteran the very first time he let me behind the wheel.

⬛━━━━━━▶

The chores Teri put me up to seemed purposefully random, as though my capacity for contrived grunt work were being measured. I worked as hard as I'd ever worked, no questions asked. Teri didn't seem aggravated when I screwed up a job. Well, that's not entirely true. She got plenty pissed. But screwing up was a minor offense compared to a single eye roll or the faintest detectable exhale of self-pity.

All right, that's it, she'd say, her voice almost merry. Summon the Wagoneer. This boy's going home to mama.

I learned to eat my woe for lunch. I learned fast because Teri's threats were never idle. She'd been firing interns since Ronald

Reagan's first term. And where would getting fired leave me? At home, fending off the neighborhood Vienna-sausage eater, sparking joints instead of fuses.

On the Thursday of my first week, I spent the morning with a recently promoted engineer. Together, we lugged the contents of his cubicle up a flight of stairs to his new office. As soon as we finished, I looked up to see Teri coming down the hallway. She had an uncanny way of showing up just as I finished something.

She handed me a bag of blue urinal biscuits.

Drop one in every butt hut, she said. Then she was gone.

————————

I knew of only one portable toilet on the whole property, a faded green one beside the main road. But Teri had given me six urinal biscuits. Fearing hesitation would be mistaken for laziness, I started hiking. It was all downhill. The temperature hung in the low 100s. A few trucks drove by, spitting dust and gravel. Not once was I offered a lift. Teri had probably made a threat over the radio: no abetting The Boy. (This had become my unofficial call sign. As in, anyone sees The Boy, send him to my trailer. Or, no more feeding The Boy leftover donuts!)

I walked along the road, not in any hurry. I needed to think of a way to find the remaining butt huts. Was this a quixotic quest? Another one of Teri's trials by humiliation? Maybe she just wanted to see me roam the property in a dehydrated delirium, stashing urinal biscuits like Easter eggs among the sagebrush. And then fire me.

As I reached the hut I got an idea. It was such a good idea that I had to pee, and I nearly forgot to leave behind a biscuit before starting back.

————————

Sticky with sweat, I welcomed the dry push of AC when I came through the main door. Maggie looked up from the receptionist desk. I set down my sack of biscuits and sauntered over to the large aerial photo of the quarry.

How long ago was this picture taken? I asked.

Last summer, Maggie said.

My pinky was already tracing the main road up the hill from the highway. And there it was: a practically unnoticeable, and yet unmistakable, white square beside the road where I'd just been. Never has *Highlights* magazine provided a boy with a more rewarding seek-and-find. From this bird's-eye view, I hunted every millimeter of that photograph for similar white squares. I found three right away, then a fourth. I couldn't find the fifth, so I took a more systematic approach, raster-scanning the whole photo with my finger. And there it was, a white square so close to a building I hadn't noticed it before. If these five butt huts hadn't been relocated since last summer, I was golden. I also had some hiking to do. Two of the huts were in Section A, one in Section C, and two more in Section D. I'd never been outside of Section I.

I chugged half a dozen Dixie cups of water from the conference room cooler and set out. About a mile down the road I came upon a chain link fence with a sign on it: BLAST ZONE. NO ADMITTANCE WITHOUT PROTECTION. I froze, weighing my options, then turned and walked all the way back to Maggie's desk.

I think I need some kind of protection, I said.

Don't fret, sweetie, she said. Teri's bark is worse than her bite.

Maggie took a key out of her desk drawer and unlocked a closet stocked with hard hats. She handed me one and I tried it on. It came down over my eyes, but she showed me how to adjust the inner webbing so it fit. She took a radio off the charger and twisted the knob. It beeped to life.

Take this along, she said. Stay on channel two.

I thanked her and went back out into the heat. I walked until I came once again to the fence. After pausing for a moment to look around, I carried on, following the road until it crested at the rim of a canyon.

Before I could see the quarry, I heard it: intermittent engine revving, back-up beeping, pneumatic groans and exhales, and the unnatural scuffing and squeaking of rock against steel. The wind kicked up dust, reddening the sun and making the landscape feel Martian. From afar, the heavy machines resembled insects, some digging with long proboscises, others crawling like centipedes.

I descended on switchbacks, staring as I walked at the gaping hole on the opposite side of the canyon. The hole was C-shaped and measured about a quarter of a mile across. The earth had been formed into steps, each as high as a house, like an amphitheater for giants. Various materials had been sorted into piles near the mouth of the hole: boulders, gravel, dark soil, light soil. The insects tended to these piles.

The relative scale of things reversed as soon as I neared the action. Suddenly I was the bug. The tread marks in the road were ankle-deep in places.

I raised a hand to my brow and surveyed the area, breathing easier once I'd spotted all five of the butt huts—right where I'd expected them. I set off toward the closest, making sure to stay off the road to avoid being run over, loping like a deer over sagebrush.

TWENTY

I may have taken more pride in my newfound job than it warranted. Give a starving boy a urinal biscuit and he'll make a feast of it. But by merely surviving the quarry for a few days, I'd accomplished something. The place could just as well have been Mars for how removed it looked and behaved compared with the world I'd grown up in. The land did not seem to belong to nature as I understood nature. It had no lakes or streams or forests, no hiking trails or camping spots. It was hardly photogenic or photosynthesizing, home mainly to craggy species of plants, animals, and people with low standards of what consisted of living. I couldn't wait to get back out there every morning.

Meanwhile, riding home those first few evenings in the Wagoneer was like re-entry. It took time to fully decompress. We'd re-emerge from the desert into the Truckee Meadows' tree-carpeted valley and head toward its center. Along the way, we passed the school where I'd eaten lunches in the bathroom, and the Atkinsons' house, where Kelly and I'd fogged over our issues in pot smoke, until finally docking in the garage of 1525 Moore Drive, a house I'd all but ruined. Still, all these places were quickly becoming historical landmarks, belonging to the past, not the present. With each passing day, the settings of my recent crises were losing their power to bum me out. Compared with the sprawling plateaus and bombed-out mountainsides of the quarry, everything else seemed smaller in much the same way that the once-massive playground equipment at my elementary school shrunk to comical proportions when viewed from my now-bigger body.

I kept such thoughts mostly to myself. They seemed safer in my possession. If I never spoke them they could not be refuted, corrupted, or stolen.

One night at dinner, Dad asked how things were going at work.

Pretty good, I said, stuffing steak in my mouth to avoid elaborating.

What've they got you doing?

I kept chewing and looked to Mom.

Go on, she said. Tell your father what you're doing.

I washed the steak down with milk. Maintenance mostly, I said.

Dad set down his fork and knife. Oby, you're there to *learn*, he said. Right? They should know you're an intern, not a janitor.

That's exactly what I told him, Mom said. I refuse to drive him out to the middle of nowhere every day so he can unclog toilets.

I chewed. While I fully agreed with my parents in principle, in practice, things were more complicated.

I think it's time we call the quarry, Mom said. Get this Teri on speakerphone, you and me and your father. Set things straight.

This, of course, was something I could never allow to happen.

No, I said, my voice firmer than I'd expected. I'm working my way up. On my own.

My words were meant for Mom but my eyes beseeched Dad. I knew he'd understand somehow, man-to-man, what became of newbie quarry boys whose mothers called to complain.

I don't know, Mom said.

Dad picked up his fork again and stabbed at a potato wedge. He didn't lift it to his mouth, just let it hover over his plate.

Oby's hardly been there a week, honey, he said. We could give it some time.

Don't *honey* me, Mom shot back. You're not the one shuttling him back and forth.

Dad tilted his head to the side noncommittally and put the potato in his mouth. He chewed, swallowed, repeated. Mom groaned and stood up from the table, dropping her napkin on Dad's head on her way to the kitchen.

I don't mind the work, I said. Calluses build character.

Dad perked up. He took the napkin off his head. Who told you that? he said.

Teri did.

Yeah? he said. He raised his voice: You hear that, honey? You hear what your oldest son just said?

I looked down at the carpet to conceal the pride on my face. I wanted this feeling all to myself. I hoarded it. This was *my* stand I was making. Still, I could tell Dad was happy. He started nodding to himself.

I like this Teri fellow already, he said.

———————

Mom hoped.

Dad, though, somehow already *knew*.

And what they hoped/knew was that my job at the quarry would impact me indelibly. Until this point in my life, the things I'd done had risen to the level of "activities." Boy Scouts, Academically Gifted class, tennis camp—these were wholesome and worthwhile and formative, but, they amounted to dabbling, really. They were the realm of boys.

The quarry was man's territory.

I'd made mistakes. I'd had misadventures. But the more Dad talked to me about the quarry that first week, the more I allowed myself to open up about it, despite my superstition about saying such things aloud. I think it was the look in Dad's eye, like he knew what I was getting for my birthday, but didn't want to spoil the surprise. I wonder if he saw the door that separated what I'd been from what I might become and, like a bouncer convinced of my credentials, decided to stand aside to let me through.

He didn't always make a point of saying goodnight to me, but one night that week he came into my room and stood beside my bed looking down at me. The only light in the room came in through the hallway door.

I'm proud of what you're doing, Oby, he said.

I haven't done anything, really.

Well, it's an internship. Your job is to watch and learn. And then pitch in whenever you can.

Yeah. It's just an internship.

No, he said, shaking his head. Look at me.

I looked up. He was backlit, a silhouette. The shadow of a full-size man projected across my bedspread.

This is a big thing, he said. You understand?

I nodded.

You can't screw this one up, he said. I mean, you still *can*. But you're not going to.

I nodded some more.

He cleared his throat. I couldn't see his face very well, but it looked like he might be smiling. Then he walked out.

TWENTY-ONE

Friday of that first week at the quarry was the day I'd been awaiting my entire life, without knowing it. No one had told me about the Friday tradition. The one indication of anything out of the ordinary came on Thursday afternoon. Teri caught me on my way out the door.

I wouldn't let Mommy pack your lunch tomorrow, she said.

I took this to mean that the time had come for a real man to pack his own lunch and so I did just that, to Mom's delight. Friday morning, I set my alarm half an hour earlier than usual, and stuffed a brown bag with all the same things Mom put in my lunches, except in less nutritious proportions. When I got to the quarry, I put this mayonnaise-laden, fruit-deficient masterpiece in the break room refrigerator, my name written large on the bag.

Maggie bid me good morning on my way out to Teri's trailer. See you at the barbeque, she said.

Right, I said, turning back to the break room. Making sure no one was around, I removed the evidence from the fridge and slipped undetected into the men's room to throw the bag in the garbage. Teri wasn't likely to come across it in there, although as I crossed the parking lot to her trailer I regretted not flushing the zip-locked food like so many baggies of cocaine. Just to be sure.

I was distracted from these thoughts by a plume of dust rising along the main road. An official-looking procession of vehicles approached. At the front, a pair of red pickups, each equipped with a siren and lights. Behind the pickups, a tanker truck of some kind, painted yellow. It had a long, tubular arm retracted along its back. They did not slow down as they passed the office complex and continued up the hill toward the quarry. I went to Teri's trailer and told her what I'd seen.

The pump truck? she said.

Yeah. The big one?

Those metal storage bins you saw on the side are bulletproof, she said. That's where they keep the boosters.

What's in the tank?

There's a partition. One side's ammonium nitrite prills. The other side's diesel fuel.

ANFO, I said under my breath. Ammonium nitride fuel oil.

Gold star, Preppy. It doesn't get mixed until the last minute, though, when they pump it down the holes.

Cool.

No, the stuff's a greasy mess. You find all the butt huts?

I think so.

And?

I saw the quarry. It's big.

That it is.

Am I going to start working there pretty soon?

Not having enough fun on this side of the fence, are we?

No, I am. It's just—

You've been here one week, Preppy.

I know, but—

One week! And trust me, you're better off with me than those union meatheads.

I know about explosives, I said. I'm careful.

Are you even listening? It's not the ANFO that worries me. You could fire a gun at that shit and it wouldn't budge.

But not the boosters, I said. Those will definitely blow.

Oh, well just listen to The Boy here! I know all about you, Oby. Yeah, you're smart. But that's not always an advantage. Those drillers—well, I'll just let you see for yourself today. They're a pack of hyenas. They'll eat you alive.

She looked me up and down, as if reassessing my stature. With a chuckle, she walked over to her truck and hopped in. I scurried to catch up.

I'm not a little kid, I said.

She ignored me as I slammed the passenger door and fastened my seatbelt. Just as she was shifting down into reverse, she leaned across the bench seat, right up to my ear...

HEY!

A reflexive spasm gripped my body for a split-second, just enough time to send my shin into the dashboard, my elbow into the door frame.

Jesus! I hissed, my voice drowned out by Teri's cackling. What's wrong with you?

Teri started to mimic me: *I'm not a little kid...I'm not a little kid.* The voice she used was unfairly high-pitched. She kept at it, recycling the words over and over, faster and brattier with each repetition until it ceased to be recognizable human speech. I had a feeling like lava pouring into my chest.

Stop, I said through my teeth.

Oh, stop! Stop!

And the lava reached the brim of me and spilled over.

Fuck off, I said. I said it without stuttering. I said it plenty loud. There was no going back. I knew, and maybe I was even pre-pared to accept, that it was *me* who was truly fucked.

Come again?

I sat in silence. The world wheeled under the hood of a Ford Ranger. I became dizzy.

Come again.

You heard me.

No, I'm not sure I did.

I'm not going to repeat it.

Oh, really? Teri said. And why's that? Because you're too much of…

I said fuck off.

Right, I thought so.

I looked across the bench seat at her, and I kept looking until she looked back at me. She smiled, but I didn't. I just kept looking at her until she looked away.

I was getting worried you didn't have any backbone at all, she said.

I looked back at the road.

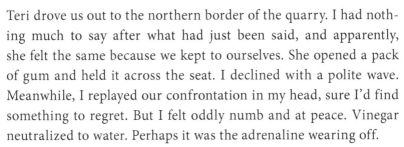

Teri drove us out to the northern border of the quarry. I had noth-ing much to say after what had just been said, and apparently, she felt the same because we kept to ourselves. She opened a pack of gum and held it across the seat. I declined with a polite wave. Meanwhile, I replayed our confrontation in my head, sure I'd find something to regret. But I felt oddly numb and at peace. Vinegar neutralized to water. Perhaps it was the adrenaline wearing off.

We rounded a hill and headed toward a swath of desert black-ened by a brushfire the previous summer. Thunderstorm runoff had eroded the soil, creating networks of trenches and undermin-ing fences along the property line. Teri parked beside some sagging barbed wire. She opened the tailgate and handed me a post-hole digger and a rock bar. For herself she took a can of orange spray paint and walked down the fence line. The can rattled when she shook it. She started drawing Xs on the ground. When she was done she came back to the truck.

I suppose you'll need to borrow some gloves, she said.

She popped the lid on the toolbox and fished around. She tossed me her pair, leather with a floral-print canvas backing. They fit my thin fingers nicely.

Without another word, she slammed the bin shut, climbed back in the truck, and drove away. I stood beside the road for a minute after she was gone. Was this punishment? With Teri, the difference between respect and indignation was subtle. Take the fact that she'd given me zero instructions. This meant I didn't need to have my hand held through every task. *Or*, it meant that whatever plan of action I took, it would be wrong and she hoped I would die.

The desert buzzed. Grasshoppers made short flights among the charred sagebrush, their wings clicking. Quail shuttled across the road. I picked up the post-hole digger and jabbed it into the first orange X. It sunk in a few inches and reverberated in my hands. I fetched the rock bar. After a few minutes I gained leverage on a rock shaped like a cashew and pried it out. Sweaty, but sort of satisfied, I took off my shirt and draped it over the fence. The sun hung high, stalled at midday. I watched a hawk ride the thermals, banking gently left and right like a kite.

Stab with the blades, spread the handles, lift, release—I succumbed to the rhythm of the post hole digger. My muscles needed the blood more than my brain. Soon doubt and speculation gave way to blisters. Cones of fresh soil took shape beside each hole. One by one, I devoured Teri's Xs.

Teri returned about an hour later with a few bags of concrete and a 5-gallon jug of water. The truck hummed with the extra burden of the air conditioner. I had the rock bar jammed under a particularly stubborn rock. I left it there with its long handle angled skyward and walked over to the truck. On the way I picked up my shirt off the fence and draped it over my shoulder. Teri leaned against the truck bed, watching me approach.

Suppose you're thirsty, she said.

A little, I said, sliding the jug onto the open tailgate. Squatting down, I put my mouth up to the spigot and drank. The water was warm and tinged with the taste of plastic. Teri watched as it spilled down my chin. I wiped my mouth with my shirt and drank until I had my fill. And it was only after I'd let out a sated *ahh* that she chose to mention the thermos of iced tea in the truck.

No thanks, I said.

I pulled a bag of concrete down from the truck and flipped it over to read the mixing instructions. Teri had her arms folded on the rail. She seemed in no hurry.

You're just like my little brother, she said.

Yeah? I said, realizing I was going to have to humor her. How old is he?

Nine years younger than me.

How old are you?

How old do you think I am?

I don't know.

Guess.

Okay, I said. Thirty-five.

What!

Thirty-eigth?

You're fired.

C'mon. *You* asked. I'm not good at this.

Thirty-eight? Jesus, do I look that old? I've been out in this damn desert too long.

I backpedaled.

You don't look that old.

Oh, now *that's* the way to smooth talk a lady!

I didn't know that's what—

Never mind, she said. Forget it.

Sorry. How old *are* you?

Not as old as I look, apparently.

You look younger than my mom, I said.

Keep digging, she said.

The Friday barbeque was well underway when Teri and I arrived at the scale house, which wasn't a house at all, but a booth. Trucks coming into the quarry were weighed here on pads built into the concrete, weighed again on their way out and billed for the added mass. Behind the scale house was a patio with an awning, picnic tables, and a charcoal grill. Bill was standing at the grill wearing an apron. He used a spatula to peek under patties, their drippings exciting the fire below. He and Tom, the quarry manger, were talking when we walked up.

Hope you're hungry, Oby, Tom said.

Starving.

Teri not feeding you? he laughed. Though, you must be doing something right. It's Friday and you're still around.

Teri's gone soft, Bill said.

Teri popped a grape in her mouth. Chewing, she nodded at me and pointed to the ground. Heel! she said.

Tom and Bill raised their eyebrows, watching to see what I'd do. I put on my best hangdog expression and waddled over to stand at Teri's side. This made even Teri smile.

I hadn't met everyone at the quarry yet, so Teri ushered me around, making introductions. The quarry's four resident females, not counting Teri, sat smoking together at a table in the shade, ashing into a common cup. I knew Maggie from the front desk and had seen Denise around the office; Karen and Loretta were new faces, both of them scale operators. Teri called this foursome The Hens. They smiled up at me, exhaling smoke in courteous directions.

This is The Boy, Teri said.

They extended limp hands for me to grip and started in immediately with personal questions, talking over each other, hardly waiting for my answers, muttering asides I couldn't hear. Amidst it all, Loretta asked whether I had a girlfriend.

Not right now, I said.

I see, Loretta said, her voice raspy. You're keeping your options open, good.

Smart, Karen said, tapping a long purple fingernail against her temple.

Oh, this one's smart all right, Teri said. He just doesn't know shit.

Kind of cute though, Denise said.

She winked at me. The other three looked me up and down, coming to their own conclusions.

Easy, ladies, Teri said.

Oh? Loretta said, startled. This one yours, Teri?

Just for now, I said. I might go work with the drillers.

Teri shook her head.

Drillers, Loretta muttered, taking a drag. Good for one thing.

Loretta blew smoke. Ain't they all? she said. Oby, don't ever become a man.

How do you know I'm not a man? I asked, feeling perky.

Oh, my! Loretta said. We got a live one…

I felt Teri's hand against my back, guiding me away from the table. I glanced back over my shoulder. The Hens had already resumed chatting, but Karen noticed me and waved coyly. Not to be outdone, Denise pulled the cigarette out of her lips and blew me a kiss.

Teri led me over to meet the two engineers and the quarry accountant, a trio she called the Brain Trust. As we approached, the accountant scurried away. The engineers stood guard at the ice chest. One was short and the other tall. Both of them wore short-sleeve work shirts tucked into sensible jeans. Both were drinking Diet Pepsi.

Gentlemen, Teri said.

Teri, they said.

She brushed past them on her way to the ice chest. I helped myself to a Dr. Pepper. Teri took a water.

This is Oby, she said.

Yeah, the short one said. He helped me move into my new office.

Corner office, said the tall one.

They're all corner offices, the short one said. But the view's the same in every one.

Desert, moaned the tall one. Desert, desert, desert.

Plenty of engineering jobs in the city, gentlemen, Teri said, if you don't like it here.

Teri turned away and the tall engineer gave me a look. It was a look I'd already begun to recognize. It asked, *Is she for real? Are you with her or me on this?*

I was learning a look of my own for such situations, a shrug/smile combo that offered no hint as to my allegiance. It said, *Teri's Teri.*

Next, I met the muckers, all four of them. A squirmy breed, mole-like with beady eyes and pudgy faces. Muckers spend their days wielding 40-foot hydraulic arms, filling their hands with seven cubic yards of earth at a time and their ears with nothing but Rush Limbaugh. A life insulated from nuance. The world breaking down into types of rock. Barbeques must have been torture for the muckers, forced to climb down from their air-conditioned cabins and mingle.

I nodded to them. They nodded back, cautiously. One of them had the brim of his cap so tightly curled around his face that I could not be sure he even had eyes.

The muckers, Teri later explained, are crazy fuckers.

Having made the acquaintance of The Hens, The Brain Trust, and The Muckers, there remained but one clique to confront: The Drillers.

About a hundred yards from the scale house was a wastewater pond. The pond was surrounded by desert, save for a patch of lawn on the near side. All five drillers were there sitting on lawn chairs. A row of fishing rods protruded from the lawn near the shore. Each rod was kept upright by a spring-loaded mechanism attached to a spike driven into the turf. The lines led out to red-and-white indicators bobbing on the surface of the pond. As Teri and I approached, one of the men turned around in his chair, followed by the other four. They stared at us. I recognized Jack from the conference room.

Let me do the talking, Teri muttered while we were still out of earshot.

When we reached the lawn, the men stood up from their chairs.

Boys, Teri said.

Teri, they mumbled.

I wanted to introduce you to The Boy.

We've met, Jack said, looking down at me.

I shook their hands in turn and did all I could to keep my

mouth shut, my face flat, and my eyes dead. I didn't want them to read into me. I became a hardened shell of a boy, with guts of either angel food cake or black powder, so take your chances. Fuck with this boy at your own peril. Oby the Kid.

Say, Arnie, Teri said. How's that pretty wife of yours doing?

No, Arnie said. Did she call here again? Goddamn if I didn't tell her...

No, no, Teri said. She hasn't called in a while.

One of the rods started to jitter. It bowed toward the water.

Fish on! Jack said. He set his hands on Teri's hips and gently scooted her aside, the way a man leads a woman in a waltz. Had this been a ballroom instead of a quarry, or had Teri been any other woman, Jack's gesture would have amounted to chivalry. Teri slipped the embrace and squared herself to Jack, but he was already jogging toward the bank. He unclipped his rod from its base and set the hook with a sharp whip of his arm. He started reeling. A fish thrashed for a moment at the surface of the pond, prompting whoops from the drillers. In less than a minute, Jack had landed the fish and we gathered around to have a look.

Looks like Belvedere, Arnie said.

No, one of the other drillers said. That there's Ted Nugent.

Sure as shit, said Jack. The Atrocious Theodocious himself. See, there's that scar across his back from that time Hector foul-hooked him.

Ted Nugent was one of a few dozen largemouth bass whose sore lot it was to occupy this particular wastewater pond and to mistake a waterlogged worm for a lucky meal a few Fridays a year. Jack pried the hook out of Ted's jaw with the pliers of a rusty Leatherman and held him aloft by his tailfin. The fish dangled over Jack's awaiting gullet.

Don't worry, Teri, Jack said. This ain't meat. Just fish.

Let the poor bastard go, Teri said.

Yes, sir.

Jack hurled Ted like a boomerang out over the water, granting the fish, with each uneven revolution, dizzying aerial views of his landlocked home. A small splash and Ted was gone. Again, the drillers laughed.

Already I could see the truth behind Teri's analogy to hyena. These men had crooked smiles and sunken eyes. Their bodies were muscular in some places, bulging with fat in others. Slouching, howling scavengers who howled with delight at one another's follies. On an individual basis, the drillers were awkward. Quiet. Pathetic. As a pack they ruled the landscape. Eating indiscriminately, mating opportunistically. Even Teri tended to cower in the presence of the pack.

Come on, Oby, she said. She turned to go.

I think I'll stay, I said. I wanted Teri to see that I could survive an encounter with these animals. Plus, I'd spent the afternoon digging holes with my shirt off. I'd earned the right to fraternize with fellow excavators.

Jack spit. Save some carrot sticks for us, he said.

Teri was looking dead at me. She said not a word.

Jack's limp index finger snapped against the Copenhagen can each time he shook it. Cupping the can inside his massive hands, he gave a gentle twist. When he lifted his hand the lid was gone, palmed like a magician's coin. He held the can up to me. What looked like coffee grounds had been packed into a perfect half moon. A sweet aroma wafted out.

How much do I take? I asked.

The other drillers chuckled. Jack shushed them.

Pull out your lip, he said, and I did. He pinched a wad and set it against my gums.

Pack it down with your tongue, Arnie said.

Like thith? I lisped.

Yup, Jack said.

The taste: unidentifiable. Saliva gushed, and I spit. Before long my jaw began to tingle. The drillers returned to their row of chairs and I took a spot at one end, sitting Indian-style in the dry grass. They kept an eye on their rods and spoke very little. My heart wanted to beat its way out of me. I took a deep breath and stared at my boots, which were floating in and out of focus.

How is it working for Teri? one of the drillers asked.

His name was Guy. As usual, I strove for ambiguity.

It's fine, I said.

She wasn't always such a hardass, Guy said. Old Jack'll tell you.

I looked to Jack. The muscle in his jaw tightened, relaxed.

Jack and Teri, Guy continued, those two got *history*. They used to live together in a little house up the road, past Arnie's place. Both of them worked at the quarry. She worked in the main office. Cute little biscuit. Long hair, big eyes... Anyhow, Mr. Sullivan— the old guy who used to run this shit hole—he took a liking to her. Made her his deputy. And toward the end there, he got sick and pretty soon she was calling shots, bossing folks around. He'd just sit in his big old leather chair and laugh and cough and say, do what Teri says, except of course he called her Barbara. That's her real name, I think. I forget.

Guy stopped and looked to Jack.

That's right, Jack said.

It rubbed you wrong, huh, Jack? Getting bossed by your old lady?

Jack spit.

Guy looked back at me.

It bothered *all* of us, he said. Jack and Teri, they were always yelling at each other. Mr. Sullivan wanted to get her an office but she asked for a trailer instead. Wasn't long before she stopped riding home with Jack.

Moved into the goddamn trailer, Arnie said. Got a bed in the back room.

Interesting, I said.

My summarization earned a mumble of affirmation from the row of chairs. I tried to sit still despite the sudden onset of influenza symptoms. The ground felt watery. My hands shook. Someone yelled for us to come and eat. The drillers got up from their chairs and made their way back to the patio. I followed briefly in their wake, but slipped away. I knew firsthand the location of the nearest butt hut.

The air inside the hut was humid with the vapor of human effluence. It must have been one hundred and twenty degrees in there. I barely had time to lock the door before I puked down the hole, splattering the toilet seat. I steadied myself with an arm against the toilet paper dispenser. And there I stood for quite some time, dry-heaving and spitting and trying not to stare at the mash of partially digested Life cereal slowly diffusing into the blue sludge.

I heard Teri desperately shouting my name. I opened the door and saw her jogging up the road. When she saw me, she threw up her hands, not so much relieved as disappointed. I started to speak but she raised a hand to shush me and un-holstered her radio.

Found him, she said.

Roger that, came the response. We'll stand by.

Negative, Teri said. All present and accounted for. We're a go.

Ignoring me, she turned and walked back up the road. I ran to catch up. Moments later there came a sound like a cracking whip, nearby at first, and immediately receding. Then, BOOM! A smash-up of massive proportions. Rolling thunder over roaring ocean. The ground trembled and was still again. Then, what sounded like a hailstorm.

I left Teri and ran back to the barbeque. When I looked beyond the pond to the quarry, I saw in its place a dust cloud from which startled birds were emerging, squawking as they fled.

TWENTY-TWO

After a shot, the quarry cliques scatter.

The drillers' job is done for the week. So, they whoop and fight and mount their hogs and ride out, the sounds of backfiring V-twin engines growing ever-fainter as they descend from the quarry foothills. By sunrise Monday, untold cocktail waitresses will have been groped and pool halls pillaged, Reno's dark-hour delights savored, sucked on, and spit out.

The muckers' job, meanwhile, begins anew. They climb back up their bulldozers, excavators, and crushers, and they muck. Before next Friday the pile must be sifted and sorted, dirt painstakingly transformed into *material*.

The Brain Trust slips back to the office to pore over survey maps and spreadsheets.

The Hens return to their roosts.

Teri and I stuck around to clean up the barbeque. Tom attacked the crusted grill with a metal brush. He chatted with Teri about operational details and upcoming projects. My appetite returned. I grazed on potato salad and sun-warmed watermelon wedges, then happened upon the remnants of a birthday cake. I zeroed in on a choice corner piece lopsided with frosting. Teri got a call on her radio. One of the muckers sounded distressed.

We had another rogue out here in Section B, he said. Did some damage.

Teri cursed into the wind. Get in the truck, Preppy, she said.

You've got to try this cake, I said, chewing my gooey cud.

I hate cake, she said.

A pair of muckers stood on the side of the road. They were eyeing a boulder the size and shape of a rowboat. The boulder was still damp, with clumps of fresh soil in its crevices. Teri sneered at it then walked up the road to a crater in the asphalt. She stood inside the crater with her back to the blast site and pointed straight ahead. The trajectory was easy to visualize. Having flown about 200 yards, the boulder hit the road, bounced off an embankment, and rolled another hundred feet or so before bashing in the left-front fender of a Ford Ranger.

Who parked this here? Teri asked.

One of the muckers raised a hand as high as his chin. He apologized to Teri.

Damn it, Teri said. This is inside the radius. Of course, it's not completely your fault. You're not the ones who stand around yakking while 60 pounds of ANFO goes down a 30-pound hole!

Teri took off her hat and wiped her face on her shirtsleeve. She ordered the boulder hauled away.

Got another hammock to hang? asked the acquitted mucker.

Just get it off the road, Teri said. She got down on all fours to inspect the dented fender. The wheel well had buckled to within inches of the tire.

Can it still drive? I said.

Sure, she said. So long as all the turns are right turns.

She gripped the lip of the fender and tugged a few times with all her weight. The truck rocked on its suspension, but the metal could not be unbent.

This fender needs to come off, she said. Fetch my tools.

I jogged up the road and got the toolbox. I brought it to her and set it at her feet. She stepped over it and walked back to her truck.

Get that horse back to the stable, she yelled. Keys are in it. If you need help, call your new fishing buddies.

And for the second time that day, she left me on the side of the road.

That fender was tenacious. After an hour, I'd managed to remove all but one of the bolts as well as some of the skin from my knuckles. The fender had compressed around this one last bolt and its footing was bent; I could hardly get a wrench on it. And if I did, the space wasn't big enough to get a decent grip on the handle. Leverage was hard to come by. What I needed was a Sawzall to cut away the metal. I lay on my back under the truck, trying to get one good tug, enough torque to loosen the bolt so I could maybe finish it off with my fingers.

A bulldozer rolled up. I wriggled my head out from under the bumper and squinted up at the mucker. He smirked at me, then lowered his shovel so that the blade was flush with the ground and took a run at the boulder. He scooped it and hefted it high. A flapper on the exhaust pipe opened to release a column of black smoke, then slapped shut. The mucker steered over to the side of the road and with a flick of his wrist tilted the shovel, pitching out the boulder. When it hit the ground, I felt the thud transmitted through the ground into my body.

Perhaps I should have been inspired by this matchup: a bulldozer, that bright yellow homage to mechanical advantage, versus a boulder, that most inanimate of objects. Hydraulic muscles and lever arms made a mockery of gravity. Was this a chance to gain insight into my own predicament with the stubborn bolt? A hint? *Hey, kid: try the breaker bar in the socket wrench case. Buy yourself some leverage.*

Perhaps.

As it was, my inspiration was to come *after* the rock hit the ground. Blame DNA, blame my parents, blame Reno, blame that crazy mucker. Who really recognizes their many muses?

With his front wheels still turned to the right, the mucker put the dozer in reverse and backed up. This reoriented the dozer to the left. Now facing the direction from which he'd come, the mucker threw her into forward gear and with a final burp of exhaust headed down the road again.

I waved my wrench to him, a grateful smile on my face. I found two of the bolts I'd already taken off and ratcheted them back onto the fender. Then I packed up Teri's tools and climbed in the truck. The engine started right up. The truck was parked facing north and I needed to go south. No problem. I shifted into reverse and cranked the wheel to the right, executing a three-point turn in the middle of the road. Successfully southbound, I made my way back to the stable. Whenever the Ranger crept too close to the shoulder, I'd come to a complete stop, turn the wheel to the right and back up, setting us on track again.

I didn't see Teri again until Monday.

Why'd you put that goddamn fender back on that goddamn truck? she asked.

Never took it off.

Don't lie to me, Preppy.

Why would I?

Teri considered this. Well, that Ranger doesn't go left. I tried this morning. Wheel well's still all smashed in. So, fess up. How'd you get that truck back here?

Carried it.

Wow, she muttered, playing along. All by yourself?

No. The drillers helped.

I'm sure, she said. Turned their Harleys right around to help an intern in distress.

I lifted my shoulders and my eyebrows in unison.

Fine, Teri said. Leave it your little secret. But you've still got to get that goddamn fender off that goddamn truck before we go to the pick-n-pull.

When are we going?

As soon as you get that goddamn fender off that goddamn truck.

Can I use the Sawzall?

If necessary.

⸺⸺⸺

The four-cylinder, eighty-six-horsepower Ford Ranger may very well have been damned by God. Scrawny, gutless, and doomed from its inception to slow lanes and pathetic payloads, it should never have been built. Funny thing is, Ford cranked out scads of Rangers, which was lucky for us. The saving grace of America's most half-ass pickup is the bounty of scrap parts available at junk yards. For every Ranger still on the road, there's at least one off of it, propped on blocks and partially cannibalized at your local junk yard.

The three big yards in Reno gave Teri a call every time a Ranger died so she could swoop into town and pick over the fresh carcass. Through the years, she'd filled an entire shed at the quarry with spare parts. Transplants postponed the inevitable shooting of every horse in her stable. But there weren't any fenders in the shed, so we were off to Reno.

I truly hope you didn't put that fender back on as a joke, Teri said once we were on the highway, where smoother asphalt made for smoother conversation. Because that would be disappointing, she said.

Really? I said, and I told her about a magic show I'd once attended with my uncle, who afterwards revealed to me how some of the tricks worked.

Ruined the mystery, right? she said.

I don't know, I said. I thought the show was kind of stupid. But once I knew the secrets, it wasn't. It was better, I think.

Magic?

I guess so. Yeah.

She looked at me with her head cocked. Oby Brooks, she said, you're either going to blow yourself up or become some famous scientist. Maybe both.

We sat in silence for a minute. The fact that she'd chosen to use my real name left me so assured of our tightening bond that a confession spilled out.

I want to win the Nobel Prize, I told her. That's why I came to work at the quarry.

Same here, she said.

I stayed in the truck while Teri went to parley with the owner of the junk yard. She left her wallet on the dashboard. I unfolded it and hastily catalogued the contents, taking special note of the license of one Barbara Jean Turson, a smiley organ donor with structurally remarkable bangs and doe eyes who, in the intervening decade or so, had become *Teri*. I checked the DOB and did the math. She would be turning 30 in August.

Teri came out of the office and got back in the truck. Wordlessly, she started the engine and shifted into reverse. She draped her arm over my headrest as she backed up.

What? she said.

Do they have any fenders?

We'll see.

A man in coveralls waved us through a gate and we idled into the yard. The cars were organized in long rows, open hoods like tombstones. Another man with a screwdriver in his hand stood beside a hoisted engine. He watched us.

Teri started whistling. She looked at me.

There's that smirk again, she said. You get laid last night?

I blurted a laugh. You only know me at the quarry, I said. I'm kind of a putz at school.

No! Mr. Smarty Pants? Mr. Sailing Shoes?

Ha ha.

I figured you'd fool *somebody* into liking you.

Not yet.

Ever?

I shrugged. She became flabbergasted, half for show.

Don't tell me you've never been kissed, Preppy…

Well, technically—

No, no. Mommy doesn't count.

Okay, I said, how about you?

That's none of your business.

She turned up the radio. It was some country song. She fiddled with the tuner knob on the Ranger's stock tape deck. Stations along the dial surfaced momentarily above the static: up-tempo ranchero trumpet notes, the pushy plea of a car salesman, Annie Lennox. Teri settled in on a classic rock station only to turn the volume down again.

Oh for Christ's sake, she said. I guess I'd say I'm in a bit of a dry spot myself.

Since Jack?

She wrung the wheel and laughed to herself.

Worse than women, she muttered. What else did those gossiping assholes say about good old Teri? Huh? That she's crazy? That she's a bitch?

They said you live in your trailer.

She scowled and turned down a row of trucks and parked in front of a primer-gray Ranger. The front fenders were intact, but the whole back end of the truck was smashed in. I wondered what had happened. Perhaps unable to maintain the speed limit, this Ranger had been rear-ended by the disgruntled driver of a real pickup towing a battleship. Teri had a soft spot for Rangers. I kept my hypothesis to myself.

Was Jack your first? I asked.

He was. First kiss, first crush, first broken heart.

Wow.

It's pathetic, right?

I don't know, I said. Not really.

Neither of us got out of the car. We were in no hurry. In our combined 43 years on Earth, we had been kissed by two boys, total. No hurry at all.

You really want to work with those animals? Teri said. You want to be a driller?

I just want a shot in the quarry.

I know you do. And I talked with Tom. He agreed it'd be okay if you started out as a chuck-tender.

No way. Seriously?

You have no idea what a chuck-tender is.

I know it's in the quarry, I said. I sat thinking, considering my good fortune, trying to keep a cork on my celebration. I didn't even smile, but Teri could tell.

I'm glad you're happy, she said.

She slouched in her seat, one hand dangling on the wheel. Oddly, I felt compelled to console her.

I thought I'd be working with you for a while longer, I said.

Yeah, well, I'm sick of looking at you all day. She opened the door with a creak and stepped out of the truck. Grab the tools, she said.

TWENTY-THREE

You're a what now? Mom said.

We were headed back to Reno in the Wagoneer. Todd sat in the backseat reeking of chlorine, his hair like mildewed straw.

Chuck-tender, I said.

I'm worried they're not taking your talents seriously, Mom said.

No, I argued. It's a special position. It's in the quarry, actually.

Sounds menial, Mom said.

Sounds gay, Todd added from the cheap seats. What's for dinner, Mom?

I haven't decided, she said into the rear-view mirror.

I want french toast, Todd said.

For dinner?

Todd and Mom carried on about the menu. I tuned them out and watched the desert hills go by. We rounded a corner and left the canyon. Reno spread out before us. The casino cluster had its lights on already, though the neon was little match for the late afternoon sun. Mom glanced over at me and patted my knee.

Let's ask mister chuck-tender what he wants, she said.

Waffles? I offered.

And that's how it came to be a breakfast-for-dinner night. Half an hour later I emerged from the back of the house showered and relaxed to find Mom in the kitchen playing short-order cook, cranking out French toast for Todd, a golden waffle for me, scrambled eggs with ham chunks for Dad, and an eggwhite omelet for herself. She found a half bag of hash browns in the freezer and quartered a cantaloupe for us all to share. She fried bacon.

It was fantastic. We devoured our individualized orders in a fraction of the time Mom had spent making them. A cool evening breeze came through the screen door as we drank the last sips of our hot beverages, chocolate for Todd and me, coffee for Dad, tea for Mom.

The moment for the family to scatter from the table was upon us. Todd and I shared a glance. He surely wondered the same thing I did: would Mom's zealousness in meal-making carry over into the impending marathon of dish-scrubbing? Usually, Todd and I did dishes, but tonight seemed above and beyond the call of duty. Mom had not been tidy. Batter- and egg-encrusted cookware littered the counters. Bacon grease was splattered on the cabinets, the stovetop, the refrigerator.

Out of the blue, Dad suggested we make a night of it and play Pictionary. Todd and I weren't immediately excited about the prospect. Family game night took initiative to get rolling—to tug the game out from whatever was stacked above it in the closet, to find the missing dice or cards or whatever it required, to pay attention as Dad reacquainted everyone with the rules—none of which sounded better than just lying down to let our feast digest.

Todd, in a moment of brilliance, agreed to Pictionary if we could play for something, and that something was dish duty.

Dad seemed open to the idea.

So, that means you and your brother are a team? he asked.

Todd and I looked at each other, then nodded our agreement. Todd excused himself to go find the game, and Mom began consolidating dishes into a stack. Dad halted her with a hand across her hip.

Stop right there, honey, he said. Don't clear a single dish. We're going to watch these punks do everything.

I heard that! Todd called from the hallway.

With the dining room table still covered in dishes, we retired to the family room to set the game up on the coffee table. Todd and I sat on the carpet. Mom and Dad took the couch.

As our turns drawing the clues came and went, I found myself watching my brother and my parents laughing and goading one another and felt as though I was reconnecting with them. Having been attuned to the sore state of my own affairs for so long, I'd stopped seeing how perfectly good things might actually be, at least on the home front. Glimpsing the scale of my self-absorption, I'd stumbled upon its boundary, even crossed over it into a state where I became fully engaged with my whole family all at once in a completely positive way. Had this happened since I nearly burnt us all out of house and home?

Todd, I could see, had come into his own as of late. He had a group of friends cooler than any I'd ever assembled, and all his swimming practice had made him strong and tan. There was even talk of a girl in his life, though he deflected all questions on the topic.

Dad seemed to have settled into his job selling insurance, and he'd even started jogging again.

And Mom had finally slowed down a little after all the running around to get the house back in order. Tonight, she'd elected to follow up breakfast with a glass of chardonnay, and was in an especially fantastic mood. She moved over into Dad's lap, where they marveled at their sons' telepathic ability to correctly interpret one another's cryptic drawings. Dad would take the drawing pad from us and inspect it for symbols or other signs of cheating, wondering how I'd arrived at *paddle wheel* when Todd had clearly drawn a stick figure with six arms.

It's a move, I explained.

A move? Mom asked.

Like in the backyard, Todd explained. Oby and I made it up. It's where you kind of hold your arms out and spin around and slap the other guy a bunch of times.

Like, in the head? Mom asked.

It's called a paddle wheel? Dad asked.

I don't know, Todd said. That's what we call it.

Mom and Dad just rolled their eyes. It didn't seem to bother them when they lost. We could hear them whispering and giggling in the kitchen as they cleaned for the next hour, acting the way they sometimes did when they came home from a party.

Todd and I just rolled our eyes.

TWENTY-FOUR

The chuck-tender is the lowest-ranking member of the drilling and blasting squad. His primary allegiance is to the drill itself, and to the chuck that holds the bit. The drill can bore holes fifty feet deep, eight inches in diameter. The drill cannot top itself off with gas, oil, and water. So who does?

Exactly.

On any given Monday, the drillers arrive hung-over, brimming with tall tales. They exchange Harleys for Rangers and head out to one of the quarry's stepped, semi-circular plateaus, called benches. The bench to be shot is determined in advance by the Brain Trust.

While the drillers curse the morning sun and caffeinate themselves, the tender fetches a can of spray paint and a six-foot pole. He lays one end of this pole at the crest of the bench, perpendicular to the edge, and at the other end hatches an X in the dirt. From this initial point he marks out a grid of about thirty Xs, each spaced six feet apart. He eyeballs the right angles.

Then the real work begins. The drill motor coughs to life. The helical blade twirls slowly enough to track the ascension of coil after coil. Each man settles into position. We had two drills and one supervisor. That was Bill. Bill stood beside the blast holes as we made them. Bill was worthless until a bearing overheated and everything went to shit. Then Bill was indispensable.

Nevada topsoil is crumbly, rife with fractures and rocks. So, once the drill has penetrated a few feet, it is retracted and the tender shovels the tailings back into the hole. This is called collaring. It's supposed to create a tight seal at the mouth of each hole, preventing minor cave-ins. More importantly, a snug collar can later prevent the loss of explosive energy through the top of the hole. Gold mines and other professional operations haul in a specially formulated mixture of sand and clay for collaring. The quarry was neither a gold mine, nor a professional operation.

Once the hole is dug, the drill is pulled out and the tender lowers a rope down the shaft. The rope has marks on it in one-foot increments, with a heavy bolt duct-taped to the end. The tender records the depth in a little notebook, data for the Brain Trust. Every so often the drill encounters a fracture deep in the ground. The drillers know a fracture by feel. They see a sudden flutter on the rpm gage or register a brief loss of compression, an interruption to the din, and the drill is pulled out so that the chuck-tender can shovel some tailings into the hole.

Does this fix the problem? Like rubbing dirt on a skinned knee.

In the end, no one really gives a shit. Sure, you can take soil samples from each hole and analyze them in a lab, then work up a complete subterranean profile and engineer the optimal sequence and placement of explosives. You can model soil fractures to ensure they do not pose safety risks. But no matter what you do, the powder trucks show up every Friday with their slurry of sweet-smelling ANFO and blow the bench to high heaven.

So, muck it. Muck it, and start again Monday.

In honor of my first week as a chuck-tender, Teri arranged for me to set off the Friday shot. The July sun dead overhead, she put her arm around me and led me from the patio to a small concrete pad. The congregated cliques followed behind in an informal procession, carrying soda cans and watermelon rinds. I walked over to a little wooden box, about the size of a Walkman, sitting on the concrete. A single line of det cord ran out of the box. (Kids: det cord is dreamy. Get your hands on some, loop it around a tree a few times and…Timber!)

I set my foot on the box, putting none of my weight on it, and did as Teri said, looking up at the quarry and not down at my foot. When I stepped down, the det cord cracked like a whip, the velocity of its detonation outracing its own sound, the explosion bifurcating again and again at the many couplings, cords like blood vessels branching out to all the holes we'd made, the energy finding first the boosters, which in turn set off the underground columns of ANFO we'd spent all week drilling and suddenly the earth lifted in a wave, left to right along the bench, booming as it rose and falling back with a long, low rumble, followed by the crackle of raining rocks, and billowing above it all a fog of dust, tiny bits of earth awoken from thousand-year slumbers and set adrift.

I had triggered a volcano with a tap of my toe.

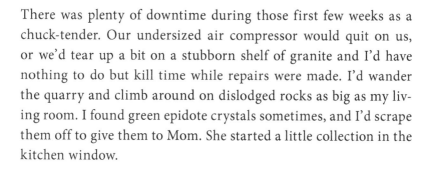

There was plenty of downtime during those first few weeks as a chuck-tender. Our undersized air compressor would quit on us, or we'd tear up a bit on a stubborn shelf of granite and I'd have nothing to do but kill time while repairs were made. I'd wander the quarry and climb around on dislodged rocks as big as my living room. I found green epidote crystals sometimes, and I'd scrape them off to give them to Mom. She started a little collection in the kitchen window.

One week, while climbing around, I came across a det cord. Following it for about twenty feet I came to a perfectly intact booster the size of a coffee can, still waiting patiently in its blast hole for the big moment. The hole was no longer vertical but sideways, and had ruptured in places. ANFO prill had oozed from the cracks.

It was not uncommon to find unspent boosters in boulders, though I'd never found one myself. Orphans, the drillers called them. Because our blast holes were not of uniform depth, diameter, or spacing, and because they were not always vertical, and because little attention was paid to the sequence of explosions, nor to the paths of the det cord, sometimes one booster would sever the det cord of an adjacent booster, or an off-kilter column would explode and blast out another column before it detonated.

I sat crouched against that crag for a few minutes. I'd heard stories about what drillers did with orphans. They waited until quitting time and took them directly to the pond to blast out some bass. I could practically hear the muddled boom of the depth charge. I could see the spherical bulging of the pond's surface and the rising spire of whitewater. I could feel the mist on my face. Yet these delicious visions were nearly spoiled by the twittering sensation in my guts. This twittering had taken root in me. It was there all day, the background of every other feeling. It flared up like indigestion. Its din grew louder in the silences, the empty moments. It had all but ruined my beloved nightly drift off to sleep.

But honestly, who in their right mind doesn't want to see a pond blow up? To hear the thuds of largemouth bass raining upon the desert? Who dares stand in the way of such a biblical phantasm?

Jesus, listen to me. Biblical phantasm? Really, Oby? I know, I know. Trust me, I know. Better now than then, even. I remain the same boy that I was on that crag, capable of romanticizing all manner of booms. I still see them in high def, hear them in surround sound, before they go off. Something I have never quite been able to do in matters of love, or lust, or whatever it is that traitorous muscle in my chest occasionally gets a mind to. When it comes to love, I'm no rhinoceros, running 30 miles an hour but seeing only 30 feet ahead. I lack the rhino's armor, his facial weaponry. In other words, I rarely charge headlong into darkness.

I reached elbow deep into the blast hole and with surgical caution, wiggled the orphan booster loose, then tugged it out. I looped the dangling det cord over my shoulder, climbed down from the rock, and set off down the road, imagining the satisfaction on Jack's face when I lay my kill at his feet. The heat had sent all living things into hiding for the afternoon, and the desert was mine. My boots made the only sound. I slipped into a walking dream. My eyes drifted into the middle distance, somewhere between the present and the future. I switched the orphan to my other shoulder and walked on, solitary, contemplative.

Oby, come in, over.

The voice hit me like a sniper's bullet. I stopped dead. I took a second or two to calm my breathing.

Go ahead, Teri?

What you got there?

I turned to see if she was following me, but the desert was empty.

Up here, she said.

I pivoted and looked to the north, where a ridge ran parallel to the road at least a thousand yards off. Parked near a cliff's edge was what looked like a Ranger. I waved my arm.

When she arrived, Teri took the orphan from me and wrapped it in a blanket. I wanted to grit my teeth and lash out at her, tell her how unsettling it was to find myself under surveillance. But riding back in the truck, I began to feel somehow relieved, and I wondered what had compelled me to take the primary road if the auxiliary would have been less conspicuous? Teri smiled at me.

Good work, Preppy, she said. You don't want to know what the drillers would do if they got their hands on this thing.

Did I detect sarcasm in her tone?

Yeah, I said, feeling like I was calling a bluff. I've heard.

What're you doing in Section B anyway? Aren't you guys drilling Section A this week?

Yeah, but the generator seized up. I had a break.

Teri shook her head. From that day forward, she always seemed to know when the drilling team was idle. Her truck would magically appear and I'd be whisked away, put on another task until the drillers radioed me. Sometimes this task was to hunt for orphans, to find them before the bad guys did. And there was always a Ranger in need of rehabilitation. Other times, though, Teri just kind of let me hang out with her.

One time I sat in on a meeting with her and a surveying equipment salesman. He tried to convince Teri that our equipment was obsolete and that we ought to upgrade to laser optics.

Our stuff still works, Teri told him.

True, the salesman conceded. But it's slow. You waste time, you waste money.

Oh, I see. We could cut costs by blowing fifteen grand on new gear.

Lasers take more accurate readings.

Teri and I smiled to each other, both of us familiar with the quarry's commitment to accuracy. A radio on the conference table chirped Teri's name. The reception was good, making it easy to pick up the urgency in Maggie's voice.

Go ahead, Maggie.

I just about stepped on another one...

With a curt 10-4, Teri excused herself. The salesman and I looked at each other. I got up and followed Teri down the hall, the salesman right on my heels.

When we reached the back patio, I could hear the rattling but couldn't see the snake. Maggie pointed it out. It was coiled under a picnic table. Guy and Arnie were tossing pebbles at it. Maggie stood near the door, taking alternating drags from a Salem and a Big Gulp. Teri chastised the drillers and tried to nudge the snake along with the handle of a flathead shovel. It swung its head to face her, black tongue probing, then uncoiled and glided toward the sagebrush. I could hear the friction of its scales on the concrete. Teri followed after it and with careful aim placed the blade of the shovel just behind the snake's head, pinning it against the ground. The snake opened and closed its jaw, making futile stabs at the air with its fangs while its body whipped and corkscrewed. Teri kneeled and picked up the snake behind its head. Its body coiled reflexively around her arm and shoulder as she stroked the diamond pattern of its skin. We all followed her around the side of the building to the parking lot, where she dropped the snake into the bed of her truck.

Thud.

Moments like this, I felt myself swell with pride. To see everyone watching her made me feel like they were really watching us. We were a duo. I was the sidekick, sure, but when Teri clapped her hands to disperse the small crowd, she didn't expect that to include me. I was with her.

The drillers wandered off, muttering jokes. Maggie lit another cigarette with trembling hands. Teri tossed me her key ring.

Escort our little guest back out to the desert, she said. Section H is far enough. Here, take my shovel. Then she looked the salesman straight in the eye and added, I'll stay here and deal with the snake.

She might as well have let the rattler sink its fangs into my forehead for all the lightheadedness and breathing difficulty this mission wrought in me. I drove to Section H with the shovel in my lap and parked beside the road with the engine running. I peered through the rear window to make sure the snake was still in the back, not waiting in ambush on the top of the cabin or something. It was coiled against the wheel well. I got out, eased open the tailgate and, standing on the opposite side of the truck bed, used the shovel handle to push the snake out the back. It disappeared over the tailgate like trash at the dump. I didn't look to see where it landed. I was already back in the cabin, shovel in hand.

As the adrenaline rush subsided, it hit me. Teri had let me drive her truck.

Teri remained my official supervisor. I had to visit her trailer for a debriefing before I went home each day, an arrangement that allowed her to keep tabs on me and, more importantly, on the drillers. Jack was of particular interest.

He's the smart one, Teri said.

That's not saying much, I said.

She laughed. Little did she know I'd become a double agent, for the drillers used me to gather counter-intelligence on the quarry's most enigmatic employee. I was one of the only people who ever entered her trailer, itself a den of mystery. The drillers craved prurient details and I delivered when I could. One time Teri left the door to her bedroom open just a crack. I caught a glimpse inside. Hanging halfway out of her dresser drawer, a bra. The lace was ragged and stained a faint yellow in places. Another time I glimpsed a candle on her nightstand.

Scented? Jack asked.

I couldn't be sure, I said.

Jack leaned against his shovel. The drill was ten feet deep and churning strong. He tilted his chin up at me.

You notice she changed her hair? he said.

Yeah, I said. Wonder why.

Reckon it's because she's a woman and her hair was too long for her liking.

I shrugged. Jack spit.

TWENTY-FIVE

I can't say for certain when it dawned on me. It may have been at that first Friday barbeque, or when I saw the DOB on her license, but at some point this idea became too much to ignore: I needed to bake Teri a birthday cake. It would be a way for me to celebrate her on my terms. She would hate this cake, I knew, unless it was extraordinary. So I sought my sensei, phoning him on a Thursday night, one week before Teri's 30th.

Dr. Pepper! he said. What's the occasion?

No occasion.

No occasion, no cake, he said.

Really, I'm just making a dessert.

Cake is not a *dessert*. Cake is a gift.

It's for a friend.

A *lady* friend?

Roger, I said.

Ah, quarry lingo? Well, cake demands precision. Attention to detail. A toothpick. Do you have these things, Dr. Pepper?

My dad has some wood toothpicks.

Be here Sunday morning around eight.

Copy that.

Over and out, he said. And he hung up.

I knew better than to eat before I went to the Weisgards'. While I doctored up a fresh stack of blueberry pancakes, they asked lots of questions about the quarry. I told them how incredible it was. I wanted Mr. Weisgard to know he'd done me right by helping me get the job. The quarry I described was nothing short of Olympian—the benches like marble steps set aglow by golden sunlight, the Rangers chariots, the drill mast a Corinthian column.

Sounds perfect for you, said Mrs. Weisgard.

And the kid still manages to find time for girls, Mr. Weisgard said.

Actually, she works there too, I said.

I see. And the young lady's name?

Barbara.

Barbara? Mrs. Weisgard said. You don't hear that name much anymore.

She's a little older than me.

Dr. Pepper here knows more about chemistry than some of my students, Mr. Weisgard said. Apparently, his taste in women is similarly *accelerated*.

I cut myself some pancake and sat chewing, swiveling slowly in my stool. Mr. Weisgard shook a finger at me, naughty, naughty.

After breakfast we retired to the study. I'd brought over a drawing to aid in the design process. Rendered in full scale with orthogonal perspectives and exploded-view cross sections, this drawing was more elaborate, and the dimensions it called for more precise, than the blast surveys we got from the Brain Trust every Monday. Mr. Weisgard was duly impressed.

Yes, he said, leaning back in his chair. I see exactly what you're after.

Mr. Weisgard, you had no idea.

———————

Chances are good that somewhere in your home is a recipe for yellow cake. It might be filed away like an old receipt. It might bear a relative's hasty handwriting. Yellow cake isn't fad food. It's time-honored. It's what we ought to think of when we think of cake. It's edible tradition. Buttery, vanilla simplicity. However, this simplicity is not arrived at simply. Consider the Standard Oil building in Chicago: this homage to sheer, rectangular verticality has no redeeming feature, save height. It is very white, and it is very tall. Simple. Yet look deeper. See the architectural legerdemain that enables a skyscraper to stand on a messy gumbo of sand and clay. Yellow cake is no different, according to Mr. Weisgard.

Everybody settles for 1-2-3-4 yellow cake, he told me. One cup of butter, two cups of sugar, three cups of flour, four eggs. Which is fine if you like your cake hard and crumbly and tasting like raw sugar.

Needless to say, Mr. Weisgard's recipe did not rely on mnemonic ratios. He copied it down for me on a piece of stationery while we baked a practice cake. He showed me how to add the milk and eggs to the batter in two stages for quicker, foolproof creaming. We folded parchment paper into quarters and cut circles to line the cake pans. Twenty-five minutes later I inserted a toothpick into our little experiment. A single crumb adhered.

Perfection, Mr. Weisgard said.

We used a Lazy Susan to add the frosting. Vanilla buttercream. When it was done he cut out a little wedge and put it in his mouth. His mustache wiggled as he chewed, humming with satisfaction.

This recipe is for high altitude, he said, so if you ever move to San Diego, call me. I'll give you the modifications.

I nodded. The prospect of ever moving away from Reno hit me like a body punch. I was only recently beginning to feel at home in my own house. I felt even more at home at the quarry. Could I yank up such new roots? Where the hell would I go? What the hell would I do there? Maybe *I* was a high-altitude recipe. I might not rise anywhere else. Too much pressure.

Mr. Weisgard cut a piece of cake to take to his wife in the next room. You want to come again next Sunday? he said. I've got a few liters of liquid nitrogen. We ought to make ice cream.

I'm in, I said.

If you don't have a date with Barbara.

Right.

Wednesday, the day before Teri's birthday, I got up early to pre-measure ingredients into little bowls. That way I could bake with television-cook efficiency later on. I left everything out on the kitchen counter, even the eggs and the butter, so it would be room temperature when I started.

The weather and the soil and the machines all cooperated that day. We bored nine holes by 4:30. As had become customary, I rode back to the stable with Jack. Even the drillers had trouble talking to Jack. Before I started working at the quarry, Jack usually drove solo. He seemed to tolerate me, though. I liked riding in his Ranger. He didn't chat me up the way most adults did. He kept to himself mostly. Either I kept the conversation going, or it would die like a motor with the choke on and we'd just listen to the wind through the windows and the empty cans of chew rattling around in the bed.

That day, though, our productivity or maybe the weather had Jack in a funny, positive mood. He had his arm out the window, his hand resting on the side mirror. He asked me about school and before long was waxing nostalgic.

Yes sir, I remember high school, he said. Chasing girls. Ditching classes. Only thing that kept me there was baseball. Had to keep a C- to play, so I studied now and then.

What position you play?

Short, he said. Sometimes second. Those are some strong memories, kid. Still smell the pine tar.

I still taste crapplesauce, I thought.

Teri used to come to my games, matter of fact. Girl was crazy. She'd sit with my parents. Made me nervous, worse than the game, knowing she was up there talking to my mom. After the games, we'd get in my truck and drive out to the desert somewhere and drink beer and watch the sun go down.

How'd you get the beer? I asked Jack.

Bought it.

Oh.

What I should have been buying were rubbers.

Until this moment, I had been staring out the window. The drab scenery on a loop like in old cartoons. No longer. I turned to Jack.

You guys had a kid?

Hell no! he said. Problem was, it took her a couple months to realize she was knocked up and a little longer before she came to her senses and took her ass to the clinic, so everyone knew. Her parents. My parents. And then everyone knew when she wasn't pregnant, that she'd taken care of it, and suddenly she's poison. My parents stopped talking to her. Hell, they stopped talking to *me*. Thought us kids were evil. But what were we going to do? Raise the thing? I didn't have a job. We were seventeen…

Holy shit, I said. Then what?

Then what? Then this, Jack said, sweeping his hand the breadth of the windshield. Teri was a mess for a while, he continued, and I was working to pay the doctors and my grades tanked. I couldn't play ball. Pretty soon, I just stopped going to class. Buddy of mine's dad was a driller. Got me a job. Teri, she stuck it out, though. Got her diploma and all that, I don't know why. The shit those kids said right to her face...

Did you start as a chuck-tender?

Jack nodded. Worked my ass off, he said, and when I turned eighteen I got promoted to driller. Rented a place of my own down the road. Teri graduated and moved in.

And the rest is history, I said.

The rest is misery, he muttered.

Mom gave me free rein in the kitchen as soon as dinner was over. I got out Mr. Weisgard's recipe, pre-heated the oven, and got mixing. First, I baked three circular cakes, each about four inches thick. They turned out nice and firm, ideal for my needs. Once a cake had cooled I took a long, serrated knife and scored around its edge, spinning the cake on the counter and gradually working the blade deeper and deeper with each revolution until at last it crossed the center and severed the single layer into two.

As I cut, thoughts of Teri ping-ponged inside my head. Thinking about Teri was one of the things I did when I wasn't at the quarry. Truth be told, I did little else. Teri was a riddle I worked at, and Jack had revealed a crucial clue. Somehow, this upset me. It had come too soon. It justified Teri. Now I saw motive where once there had been only malice. Part of me wanted the old Teri back. I could have happily drifted about the margins of her mystery for years.

Three layers turned to six. Butter turned to buttercream. Nine o'clock turned to midnight. The cake turned out better than I'd hoped. It didn't fit inside anything in the kitchen so I got a cardboard box from the garage. To reduce moisture loss, I layered the box with plastic wrap, much the way Mom once mummified her precious puzzle. My masterpiece safe in the corner of my room, I crawled into bed with all my clothes on, tired and eager for the new day.

Over breakfast, my resolve suffered blows. Dad hinted that there might be less shameless means of flattering management. Mom called my cake *cute*. Todd ducked his head behind the cereal box and acted out a convincing blow job.

The way I saw it, though, there could be no better gift for Teri. She would finally know, unequivocally, how I felt. Or at least that had been the plan. Everything showed its flaws in the harsh light of morning, and I began to fear that the old Oby was rearing his head. The pussyfooter. The second-guesser. The line-straddler. Perhaps, I was incapable of unequivocal.

Having never experienced romantic love, I could only hope that its symptoms were no more severe than whatever I'd come down with. Sometimes during our debriefings in her office Teri rested her arm across the back of the couch such that her fingers dangled into intermittent electrical contact with the hairs on my neck. I don't think she even noticed. The movies playing inside our respective heads at times like this would garner different ratings, I'm sure. I was half her age, a sexual imbecile. She had seen battle. She had procreated, then uncreated. I had no idea what I was after. But I knew that I could no longer live with diesel in my veins. I had to be defused. Teri needed to know what she was dealing with.

A baker and a bomber just use different ingredients. One, yellow cake. The other, yellowcake. Have I oversimplified? Hardly.

TWENTY-SIX

Mom dropped me and my cake off a little early.

The hell's that? Maggie said as I passed the front desk.

Samples, I said. For the lab.

The lab was nothing more than a converted bathroom in the basement with a single, dusty stereoscope on the Formica counter. The samples I'd lugged doawn there a month earlier were still on the shelf, exactly as I'd left them. I set my cake down behind some other boxes, flipped off the light and hustled out to meet the drillers at the stable.

My first fear was of being scooped, though I realized it was unlikely that anyone would know it was Teri's birthday, let alone risk calling attention to it. As if The Drillers might all sign a sappy Hallmark card; as if The Hens might treat Teri to a facial; as if The Brain Trust might pop champagne. I rode out to the benches with Jack. Steering with his knee, he slapped a can of Copenhagen against his palm a few times. We rode along, both of us quiet. He slapped the can some more.

It's Teri's birthday, he said.

I maintained my calm. Took half a breath.

She's thirty, he continued. Crazy thing is, I actually thought about getting her something. I think maybe it's these talks you and me been having. All these years at this shit hole, me and her. Holding grudges. Getting old.

What were you going to get her?

Fucking chocolates, Jack said. Who knows. She hates everything.

Yep, I said, expecting the conversation to lose steam, but he spit out the window and started in again.

What I ought to do is just say sorry to the poor thing.

For what?

Hell, pretty much everything.

The Ranger cabin closed in around me. I rolled down my window and after a few whiffs of fresh air decided to come clean about the cake.

A cake? he stammered. You're going to die!

It's not what you think. It's not a regular cake.

Don't tell me...it's got ice cream in it?

Why? Does she like ice cream?

Does she like ice cream! What I just tell you, dip shit? She hates everything!

The cake is shaped just like the quarry, I said, hoping to convince Jack I wasn't suicidal.

I also mentioned that I'd made it practically to scale. That I'd cut the six layers so as to create stepped, semi-circular benches, and sprinkled natural sugar into the buttercream to simulate desert sand.

Jack started to laugh. Not a big laugh, just a few exhales in a row. I got the message, though. He was worried for me. I was the clown prying open the bear's maw to peer inside. My predicament was at once comic and terrifying. It was irresponsible, putting myself at risk this way, and unfair to those who'd end up rushing to my aid—or, as Jack predicted, to my funeral.

I'm going to give it to her this afternoon, I said.

Just make sure everyone's gone home, Jack said. You don't want anyone inside the blast radius.

Now Jack was smiling. His tone had changed. He sounded more like a fan, the boy at a tractor pull taunting Truckasaurus's next victim as it drives into the arena.

The Ranger's engine stopped whining as we reached the crest of the canyon. A thought took shape inside of me. I tried to suppress it, to pay it no mind, but there it was. It expanded from my heart, ballooning up. It was the kind of thought I typically agonized over for weeks, but the ride was nearly over.

You still love Teri, I said, don't you?

Come again?

You do.

Jack looked away from the road at me. Just staring.

The guys put you up to this, didn't they?

Do you love her?

I'm going to kill those fuckers.

No one put me up to this, I said. I just want to know.

Jesus. You're serious, aren't you?

I'm a serious little boy.

Fucking A.

Well? I prodded.

It's complicated.

No, it isn't. It's a simple question. Do you love Teri, yes or no?

I don't know, Jack said. I guess I do. If you have to know. So, yes. I'll tell you this, though, I sure as hell wish I didn't.

Yeah, I said, turning to look back out the window.

We finished three holes before lunch without incident, and later that afternoon sunk the drill into the last of my wind-dulled Xs. I'd come to a kind of decision, though the course of action this decision prescribed remained fuzzy. I would have to improvise. On our drive back from the quarry I took my first step: convincing Jack to stay after work for awhile to help me with my surprise. He agreed to hide out in the stable. When I left him he was reclining against a pile of cargo blankets, his hat pulled down over his eyes, his hands folded peacefully over his belt buckle. I walked back to the office. My cake had not been discovered. I stopped at the supply closet on my way out the door and nabbed a pair of scissors.

The parking lot was nearly empty. I plodded across the gravel. Never in my life had I been so nervous, with the possible exception of the science fair I'd defrauded. My breath felt stunted, my heartbeat audible. Instead of going straight to Teri's door, I walked around to the side of her trailer, out of sight. I cut away the top of the box, leaving just the bottom under the cake like a plate. I stashed the top behind one of the cinderblocks supporting the trailer, then came back around to the front with the cake and knocked on the door. She yelled for me to enter, but I didn't answer. I just stepped back from the door and waited. I heard a stir, then some cursing. Many heartbeats passed.

The door opened. She stood at the top of the stairs and I on the ground, so I could see her over the top of the cake. Her eyes did a quick scan of the horizon, then fell back on me. I held the cake out farther in case she hadn't noticed it. My arms began to quiver.

For you, I said.

She looked again to the parking lot, then back at the cake.

Get it in here, she said. Now.

Actually, do you mind if we take it around back?

Just quit standing there!

She slammed the door. I turned and waddled around the side

of the trailer. Teri had an old picnic table back there. I set the cake down, quarry side out, then shook the strain out of my arms and waited. Teri came around, walking with her hands in her pockets. Her voice was almost a whisper.

Preppy, what are you doing?

What do you mean? What's it look like I'm doing?

Who told you it's my birthday?

Calm down, I said, and I told her about sneaking a peek at her license.

You should not have done this, she said. You really should not have done this.

I pointed at the cake and asked if she could tell what it was.

Is this some cruel joke? she said.

I stared incredulously into her eyes, where I swear I saw the sparkly wetness that precedes weeping. I saw it. And yet not a single drop escaped. She allowed herself one sniffle—one—and then she reeled it all in, got a hold of herself, and the show was over.

I reached into the cargo pocket of my Bugle Boys and took out a pack of Black Cats.

What in God's name…

Candles, I said.

Teri's minor episode had cracked her shell a little: she was suddenly quick to laughter. She was almost blushing.

You've got to be shitting me, she said.

Just watch.

Having laid out my share of 30-hole blast patterns, it took little time to arrange the shot. I sunk the firecrackers into the little benches so that just their heads poked out. Teri had by now taken a seat. She began narrating.

He puts the firecrackers in the cake.

I braided all 30 fuses into a single bundle about a foot in length and took a book of matches out of the cargo pocket on my other leg. Then I handed the scissors to Teri, handle out.

He hands me scissors.

For blowing out your candles. Or not. Depends if you want to make a wish.

Teri looked up at the sky.

It's tradition, I explained.

Tradition, he says. Why are you doing all this for me, Preppy? Haven't you learned a thing yet? I'm a raging bitch, you know.

A couple people remember when you weren't.

Yeah, who's that? Jack? Because I remember when he wasn't a driller.

I tore out a match and scraped it to life. The flame hissed, quieted. I lit the fuse.

You've got about 15 seconds, I said.

So, you and Jack are all buddy-buddy now?

We talk.

Jack doesn't talk.

He talks to me.

How lovely. What's he say?

I told you. He says you used to be nice. That he's been hard on you.

It goes both ways, I guess.

He got you a present, Teri. It's in the stable.

TWENTY-SEVEN

I was not there. I did not see the look on Jack's face when Teri burst through the stable door, wielding scissors and demanding a gift he didn't have. What I did see was the look on both of their faces when, a few minutes later, *I* came through the door splattered from the waist up with yellow cake and buttercream.

They were standing together, not embracing nor touching. Still, as I walked in, each of them took a half step back. I felt tension in the air. Both of them appeared relieved by my cameo. They laughed, each in their own overcompensating way. It struck me that I'd be explaining a few things to Mom when she arrived.

Teri stepped over to me and swabbed her finger through a lump of cake near my temple. Tasting it, she declared the cake delicious and invited Jack over. He found a nodule on my collar, another on my sleeve. Soon they were picking me over like chimps. Little moans, smacking lips. They sucked their fingers clean again and again. I stood by.

Good? I asked.

Oh, very, Jack said.

It was all quite weird, at least for me, especially when Jack bent down to scavenge a frosting-rich zone near my hip. But then Teri leaned in to eat a morsel right off my cheek and, before Jack straightened up, I turned my lips to hers. The connection was moist, buttery, and brief. Teri stepped back and looked at me sideways while I grinned. She shook her head. I grinned some more.

Ugh, Jack said. I think I ate some firecracker.

TWENTY-EIGHT

First kisses are supposed to unlock new realms, to lead to things, but I did not delude myself. From the moment I left the stable that day I was plotting my exit. Mom gasped as I climbed into the Wagoneer, reminding me that I was caked in cake.

I don't think I can work here anymore, I said.

What happened to the cake? Wait, did you get fired? Can they fire an intern?

I'm more afraid they'll promote me.

Tell me what happened, she said.

I'd rather not.

She looked at me crossly. I looked out the window.

Suits me, she said. I'm just about sick of this drive.

I figured Dad would have a different opinion, and so it came as a surprise to hear he too was fine with me leaving the quarry, especially since school would be starting back up in a few weeks.

You had a hell of a summer, he said. Just make sure it isn't wasted.

I asked him what he meant by that. He said that I needed to come away with a letter of recommendation.

I'm not sure, I said.

Just get the letter, he said.

I guess I could ask.

It's not a big deal, he said. People in the business world do it all the time.

The next morning, Mom dropped me off at the usual hour. Somehow, I'd awoken feeling liberated. I'd slept soundly, showered, eaten two bowls of cereal. And then I was right back where it all started, standing outside Teri's trailer. The air was cool. A jackrabbit rested on its haunches beside the stable. It kept one eye on me, assessing my risk as a predator, then licked at its paw. I took a deep breath and knocked on the door. No answer. I knocked again, and again. Silence. The knob was locked. I walked around to the back of the trailer to find the hammock empty. I sat in it.

I rocked gently, imagining what would happen if I stayed there all morning. Only Teri would ever discover me. I found this particular vantage point suited to my frame of mind: not a single tree in sight and nothing moving, canyons and plateaus, browns and yellows, some high gray clouds, a sun. Such a view cannot distract one's thoughts, only provide a barren canvas upon which to project them. I screened a highlight reel of quarry memories, edited out the rough stuff and let what little footage remained pass through the Vaseline-smeared lens of premature nostalgia.

I heard a Harley. It pulled up to the front of the trailer with its engine popping and rumbling. I stayed put. A minute later, it drove away as the trailer door opened and closed. I went back around and knocked again. The door swung open right away and there stood my Teri. Her hair was pulled back in a ponytail. One side of her collar was folded back into her neck. She nodded at me and I knew that any unprompted acknowledgment of my presence could mean only one thing…

Did you get laid last night? I asked, and she slapped me across the face. She stood in the doorway. Her mood was unreadable. My cheek was tingly.

I deserved that, I said.

And still she did not speak. I was left little choice but to elaborate on my apology, but she wasn't listening and after a while she just put her hand up.

What are you doing here, Preppy? she said. Really.

Right now?

You going to work your way up the ladder? Run this hellhole someday?

Probably not.

Of course not. You're here to get a line on your resumé.

I don't have a resumé, I said. And I like it here. I like you. And Jack, and the guys. Everybody.

That's great. Hey everybody! Oby likes us! Whop-dee-fucking-doo!

Come on.

So, we're like characters on your favorite show. Is that it? Because thing is, when you drive off with mommy every night, this show stays on. It's my life.

It doesn't have to be.

Don't give me that, Teri said, coming down from her trailer to sit on the step. Coming out here, she muttered, playing with people's lives.

I said I was sorry.

I'll admit you got us talking, Teri said, pointing up at me. You got me and Jack blabbering like crazy. Airing out some shit that's been unsaid, and it turns out we both still hate each other and love each other too. Nothing changes. Anyway, he took me to some big restaurant and pretty soon everything started pushing in on me, all these noisy people. I went into a tailspin. Next thing I knew I was pulling a Preppy, puking my guts out in the bathroom. That world, it ain't mine. Course, Jack was decent about it all and we got the hell away from there. Drove to where I could see the stars again and get my bearings. But I felt plain stupid.

It's not stupid.

I was doing fine by myself before you came. *Fine.* Now look at me.

At this, Teri shook her head and looked at the ground. This ends now, she said. You know that.

Yeah.

I can't be your boss. Not anymore.

I know.

It's been something new, I'll say that. Staying one step ahead of you. You're an allright kid. Get as far from here as you can, Preppy.

I nodded and hung my head. Would you write me a letter of recommendation? I asked.

Teri got up from the step and brushed her hands off on her jeans. She studied me. Write it yourself, she said. Maybe I'll sign it.

Fair enough.

You can borrow Maggie's typewriter.

I labored over that letter. It's a frightening exercise, recommending oneself in writing to persons unknown. The first draft relayed in detail my day-to-day responsibilities at the quarry, none of which were really impressive. So, I overcompensated on the next draft with a lot of lofty, empty, vision-statement words. I loaded another piece of letterhead into the typewriter, thinking that maybe I should write three versions of the letter and Teri could sign the one she hated least. The first one would start *Oby Brooks is the best intern that ever worked for me.* The second one would start *Oby Brooks—what a colossal fuckstick.* The third one would be some flavor in between. Gazing around the reception area, I remembered my first day on the job. Though only a few months had passed, I could already see that boy from some distance. There he was, running down a Wagoneer. See his topsiders?

Teri was right. Each night, when I left the quarry, I reentered a completely different culture. But she was also wrong, because I brought the quarry home. Its dust clogged my pores. Its heavy noises rang in my ears. And at night, I'd lie in the quiet darkness of my bedroom and close my eyes and it was always the first place my mind took me. The quarry evoked joy, dread, and angst in equal measure, a much-improved ratio for me. Really, though, this was all a delusion. It wasn't really the quarry that melted me down each day and remolded me. The quarry wasn't a place. It was a person.

The letterhead lay blank and limp on the typewriter. I knew what to write. I set loose my index fingers. They tapped out a tribute. *To whom it may concern*, it began, a salutation of mere formality. I knew exactly whom it concerned, and whom would be the only person to ever read it.

Mom would have called it a thank you note. A really good one.

Dad would have called it a letter of recommendation. And I know that's exactly what he wanted me to come away with, for myself, but that was the thinking of a different world. His world. The quarry wasn't the first rung of a corporate ladder, nor did I care to start such a climb. I loved the quarry, but even Teri understood the place was a dead end. Lucky for me, she'd taught me a three-point turn.

When I was done writing, I wheeled the letter out of the typewriter and signed it *Preppy*. Maggie gave me an envelope.

You headed over to the barbeque? she asked.

I've got some things to do first, I said.

That Teri. Runs you pretty ragged, doesn't she?

I smiled, thanked Maggie for the envelope and walked out to

the parking lot. The garage doors on the stable were open. Teri's bay was empty. I went straight to her trailer and let myself in. Never had I been in there alone. I took in the faint aroma of Old Spice and touched some of her collected objects. An epidote crystal in her windowsill cast green planes of light upon the walls and furniture. I set the letter on her desk and stepped back out into the parking lot.

A pickup truck too bulky to be a Ranger was returning from the quarry. As it got closer I could see it was leading the Friday convoy. Taking up the rear was the powder truck, its volatile load newly lightened. I stepped over to the road and put up my hand. The convoy slowed to a halt beside me. The driver of the lead pickup leaned across the cabin and rolled down the passenger window a crack.

Where you headed? I asked.

Reno, he said.

I'll never know for sure, but Teri probably hated goodbyes.

EPILOGUE

I turned thirty on Thursday. So, I survived. But instead of find-ing myself in the middle of the main drag, still buckled into an airplane seat like George Jr., I landed in a steakhouse off the beaten path. Like George Jr., I was conscious—perhaps more so than ever—and bearing only bumps and bruises.

The guys took me to the steakhouse in Mercury after work. It's the one place to eat dinner out here. Decent salad bar, good steaks. A quiet gentleman by the name of Ricardo is the only waiter, though there used to be a full staff. Ricardo wears a bowtie, just as he has every night since he came to work in the steakhouse in 1992. He's one of the few employees at the Nevada Test Site who's been here since the last nuclear test. By that time, the dry lake beds had become more like the crater-riddled plains of an alien moon. *Able* was first. They dropped it from a B-50 over Frenchman's Flat on a cold and dry January day, twenty-six years before I was born. Then came *Baker*, and *Charlie*, the names following the alphabet. But the Soviets were testing too, and in a race like that the alphabet doesn't have enough letters. They started naming bombs after rivers, mountains, scientists, small mammals, fish, birds, cocktails, cars, trees, cheeses, wines, fabrics, tools, nautical terms, colors, ghost towns, instruments, movies, horses. Bombs were dropped out of planes. They were lobbed out of balloons. They were strapped to towers. They were shot out of cannons. They were buried. The list of things engulfed by atomic fireballs here is long. One of these things was a perfectly good bank vault. Also, long is the list of things that have basked in the carcinogenic afterglow of these atomic fireballs. Eight hundred of these things were pigs.

I ate a bone-in ribeye steak with a baked potato and washed it all down with a couple of bottles of beer. It isn't often that the four of us get together outside of work but whenever we do we vow to do it more often. Ian and Clark carpool in from North Las Vegas, Macintyre from Pahrump, all three returning home each evening to significant others, though in Mac's case she's a beagle.

A sign posted on the steakhouse door beside the evening's specials reminds patrons that confidential conversations are prohibited inside the dining room. Ricardo, as usual, seated us in the corner and tried to keep his interactions germane to the menu. And, as usual, we teased him about all the state secrets he's overheard while topping off water glasses. We told him he'd missed his chance to defect and trade his information for a nice spread in Cuba. He humored us.

After dinner, we headed back outside. The sky was a purple hue, no longer sunlit and not yet starry. Streetlamps were blinking on. Warm evening winds drifted in from the desert, as if seeking shelter for the night. Ian passed around cigars. We spread out on the benches facing west and sat for a while, savoring the smoke. It was one of those nights; one of us would say something and someone would fire back or we'd laugh or no one would reply at all. Without eye contact, our conversation was freeform. Theories were proposed willy-nilly. Resolutions spoken by earnest hearts spilled into suggestible ears. Workaday minutiae were ridiculed, coworkers slandered. We gave each other the benefit of the doubt.

Rick Watson came out of his office. He waved to us but didn't come over. It struck me how unapproachable we must have looked, all slouched and smoking. I found myself wondering what a young Oby would think of the gang he'd ended up in. I'd known Ian the longest. We met in a geophysics class. I was one of two kids majoring in explosives engineering at Nevada's Mackay School of Mines. He was the other. We studied together, and usually we signed up for the same electives just so we could share the workload. He took better notes, but I had a knack for predicting test questions. Of course, I wasn't *always* right, but more times than not when a professor passed out the test I'd look over and see Ian shaking his head and smirking. Uncanny, he called it, the way we'd spend that extra half hour before class reviewing the very formulae we'd need to ace the test. I guess somewhere along the way I'd acquired a knack for staying one step ahead of grownups.

I graduated a semester ahead of Ian and went to work at the Test Site. By the time he came down, I was a supervisor, which he has yet to let me live down. Later, I hired Clark, who'd graduated from Colorado, and Mac, from a reputable explosives program at Missouri-Rolla.

I puffed on my cigar and posed a question to the evening itself: if muckers muck and drillers drill, what be we?

Rapid oxidizers, Clark said.

Paperworkers, Mac suggested.

Maybe we're flamers, I said.

Clark laughed and coughed smoke. Speak for yourself, he said. I'm married.

Of course, I took his point. I wasn't blind to the word's connotation. But that didn't keep me from wanting it for myself. Couldn't I wrest it from the lexicon? Swoop in like MacGyver and, with a tube sock and bailing wire, fashion it into something I needed?

By the way, for those curious about such classifications, I've had a few goes with girls here and there. Well, not here. Not at the Test Site, where men outnumber women nearly 10:1. (The ladies' old joke about finding a man here is that the odds are good, but the goods are odd.) Anyway, Ian and I took a couple girls to the rodeo once in college and during the fireworks, even after the fireworks, there were some fireworks. No finale though. My date never returned my calls. Then another girl, an English major (sorry, Mr. Weisgard), took me camping and talked my pants off. I lost my virginity in the pulsing orange light of a campfire while gasping for oxygen inside a mummy bag. That was so long ago I'm probably eligible to lose it again, if I cared.

I recently learned that if you rearrange the letters of Alfred Nobel's name, you get Fabled Loner. Maybe my anagram is my fate too. Oby, ever The Boy.

The guys and I were celebrating not only my thirtieth birthday that night, but a relatively productive Thursday. The Department of Energy had recently unveiled redesigned nuclear waste transportation containers. These containers were to be used in moving waste from all over America to Yucca Mountain, which neighbors the Test Site. That's where the containers would be dumped and left for Nevada to deal with for the next one million years. At least that was the plan. Well, in the wake of recent terrorist attacks, these big stainless-steel barrels were now supposed to withstand the impact of a medium-sized passenger plane and the subsequent firestorm.

Yours truly was given the enviable task of simulating such a scenario. Suffice it to say that the punch from my PETN and the heat from the two thousand gallons of spilled jet fuel it ignited sent the DOE boys scuttling back to their drawing boards. It was the third design I've had the pleasure of obliterating this year. Which begs an obvious question: do my repeated assaults on these containers amount to more than just terrific fun? Won't my exacting brutality lead to safer containers in the end, and therefore safer people? Should I be flown to Stockholm and be given a prize?

Quite the opposite. I've been lucky so far in that I've been solely responsible for most of my mistakes and rarely to blame for my successes. I remain unincarcerated and unincinerated. I live in a house I'm slowly buying with the proceeds of my proclivity in a state that never wants for things to blow up.

So, while I lack a lady, I have a hammock. On clear nights, I fall asleep in it, under the twinkling shrapnel of the biggest bang ever. All this, thanks to a cast of nurturers. Their names fill these pages. The chapters of my life warrant many thank you notes. Better yet, medals. Call them Obel Prizes. Cast them in Nevada silver. Hang them on the necks of the people who made lasting contributions, not to science or literature or peace, but to a boy.

ACKNOWLEDGMENTS

Dear Jim & Sandy Rogers, Judd & Lindsay Rogers, Tyler & Julia Rogers, the extended Rogers family from Tom and Virginia on down, the extended Bedford Family from Stew and Mary on down, Pam & Steve Hamilton, Reid and Logan Hamilton, the extended Hamilton family, Joseph & Kim Goodnight, Benjamin Clyne, David Torch, Matthew Herz, Ilsa Brink, Mena Dedmon, John & Elizabeth Leiknes, Kam & Allyson Leang, Brian Egan, Steven Malekos, Grant Korgan, Jesse Adams, Kenny Ching, Sean Ross, Keith Ganey, Ben & Erin James, Paige Dollinger, Jenny Weisberg, Stephanie Lauer, James Mardock & Emilie Meyer, Jason Ludden, Jim Smith, Melanie Perish, Paul Klein, Bob Felten, Kathie Bartlett, the UNR Spring 2007 Creative Writing Workshop, the Unnamed Writers' Group, the Quote-Unquote Book Club, Jake Highton, Travis Linn, Donica Mensing, Mikalee Byerman, Richard Davies, the Reno High English Department (Mrs. Sullivan, Mrs. Utter, Mrs. Tripp and Mr. Meschery), the Nevada Museum of Art, the Nevada Arts Council, and the Sierra Arts Foundation,

In as many ways as there are names in this overly long salutation, I am grateful. I am indebted. I say thank you, thank you, thank you for supporting me and my writing over the years. I say thank you again, even.

Dear Adam Dedmon and Gabriel Urza,
Thank you for reading and then improving just about every rough draft I've put to paper for more than a decade. You're smart and charitable critics, but above these, you're enduring friends.

Dear Michael Sion,
Thanks for taking the time to steer and cheer a young writer.

Dear Brooke Rogers,
You were supportive when there was so little worth supporting. Oby's last name is no accident.

Dear Professor Jaak K. Daemen and John Gates,
Thank you both for sharing so much of what you knew with me while I was researching this book.

Dear Sean Henderson,
Thank you for considerate and constructive editing of this manuscript.

Dear Cynthia Reeser,
Thank you for the opportunity, and for so skillfully shepherding this book along.

Dear Christine Kelly,
Thank you for welcoming Oby and me into your lovely tree house, and for taking such good care of us.

Dear Christopher Coake,

There are teachers, there are mentors, and then there is Chris Coake. You give of yourself above and beyond obligation. You set the standard.

Dear Walter Van Tilburg Clark and Robert Laxalt,

Thank you for building a literary Reno before I was even born.

Dear Sydney and Quinn,

The best books—the kind I love best—are the ones that make me want to read faster to know what happens next, and at the same time slower to appreciate every sentence. I'm finding the same to be true of daughters. I love you both so much.

Dear Jill,

What I do, we do—be it a book or a daughter or a home. Thanks for sharing this life with me. I believe in the written word, but sometimes words are too clumsy, or too clinical—the mind's loose translation of what's really going on below, in the heart. So I must ask that you please accept these words as partial repayment for so many better, untranslatable things. I love you.

Love,
Ben